KENNETH GRAHAME

THE WIND IN THE
WILLOWS

A GRAPHIC NOVEL
BY STEPHANIE PETERS
& FERN CANO

STONE ARCH BOOKS
A CAPSTONE IMPRINT

Graphic Revolve is published by Stone Arch Books
A Capstone Imprint
1710 Roe Crest Drive, North Mankato, Minnesota 56003
www.mycapstone.com

Cataloging-in-Publication Data is available at the Library
of Congress website.
Hardcover ISBN: 978-1-4965-3562-7
Paperback ISBN: 978-1-4965-3564-1
Ebook PDF ISBN: 978-1-4965-3566-5

Summary: Toad is not a bad guy. It's just that he really,
REALLY loves cars. And whenever he finds out how fast a
car can go, Toad tends to end up in big trouble.

Designer: Kyle Grenz

Printed in the United States of America.
052019 001956

TABLE OF CONTENTS

ALL ABOUT *THE WIND IN THE WILLOWS*

Author Kenneth Grahame first created his beloved characters Toad, Mole, Ratty, and Badger for his son, Alastair. The animals' grand adventures were bedtime stories for the boy, and when Grahame traveled he would expand upon the stories in letters to his son.

Grahame retired from a position with the Bank of England in 1908. He and his family moved to live on the River Thames, which became the inspiration for the setting of *The Wind in the Willows*. With characters and setting in place, Grahame completed the manuscript for his children's book. It was published that year, in the heart of what has been called the "Golden Age of Children's literature."

However, the critics were not kind, and, in general, gave the book poor reviews. But it didn't matter: the public loved the stories and the lessons they taught. One of its biggest fans was U.S. President Theodore Roosevelt. He wrote to Grahame, saying that he had "read it and reread it, and have come to accept the characters as old friends." When Roosevelt visited England in 1910, he requested to meet Grahame in person.

The play *Toad of Toad Hall* by famed Winnie-the-Pooh author A. A. Milne brought Toad's adventures to the stage in 1929. It is just one of dozens of works of art inspired by the four friends of the Thames Valley.

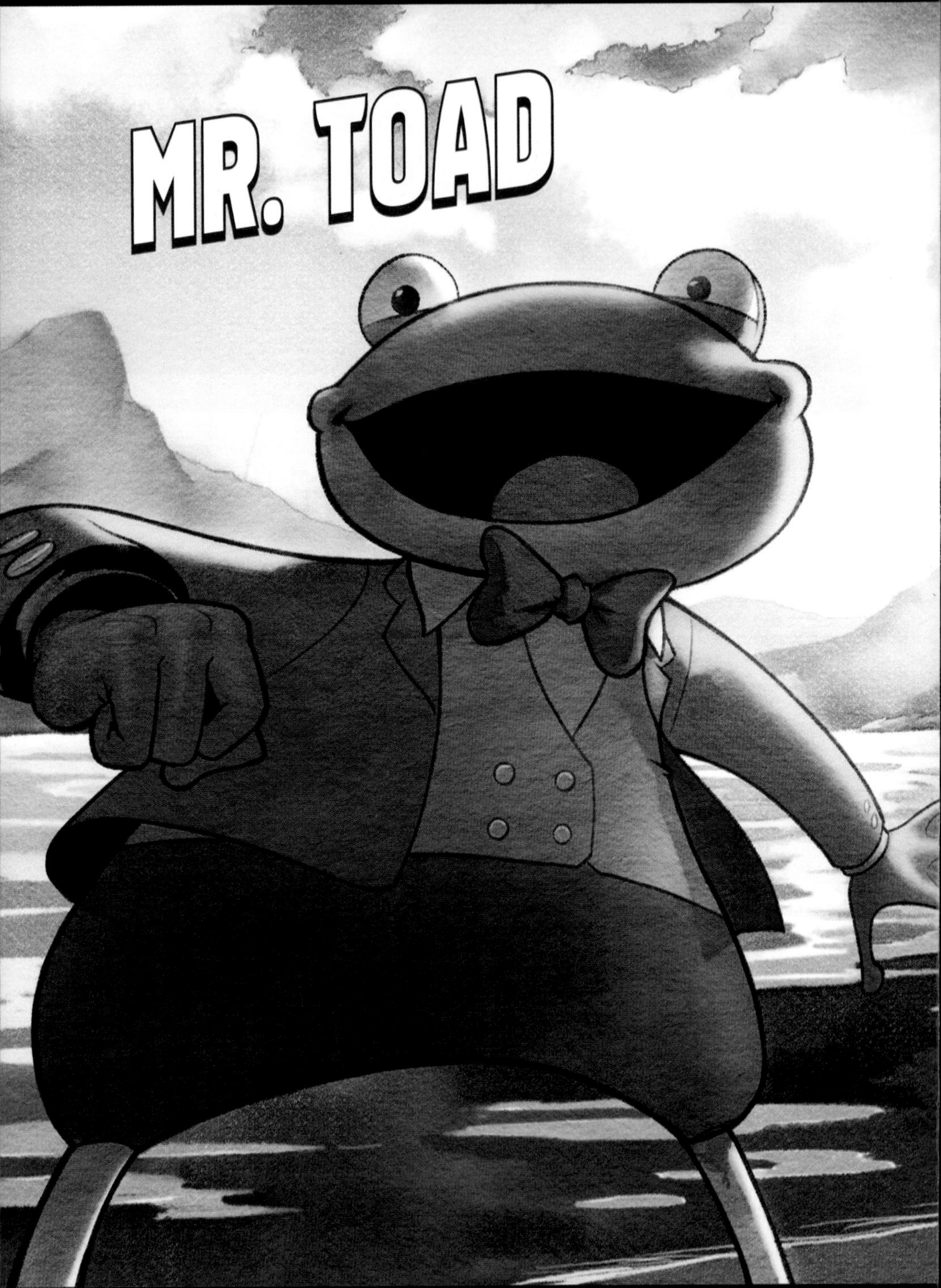
MR. TOAD

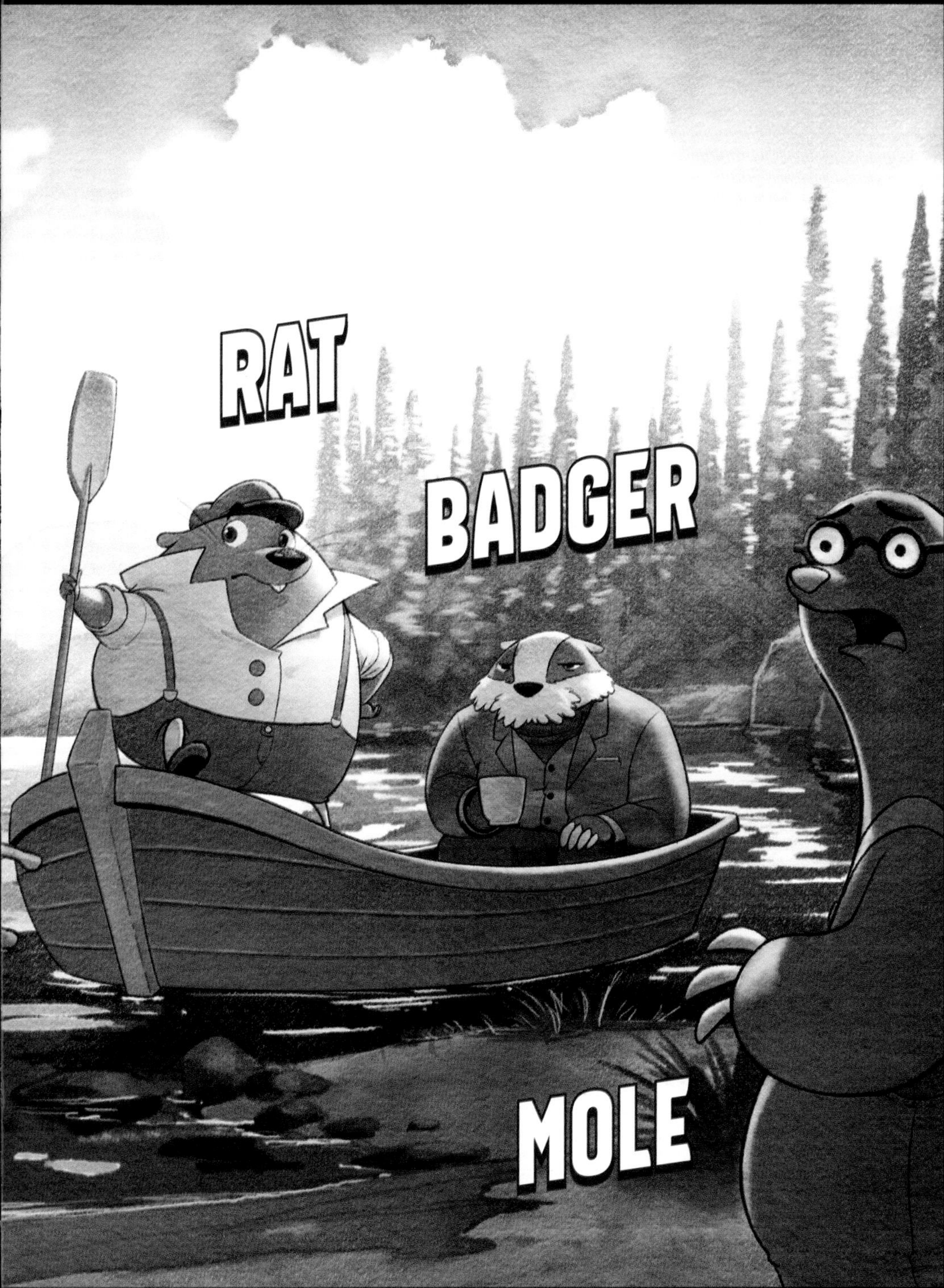
RAT
BADGER
MOLE

CHAPTER 1
THE LIFE ADVENTUROUS

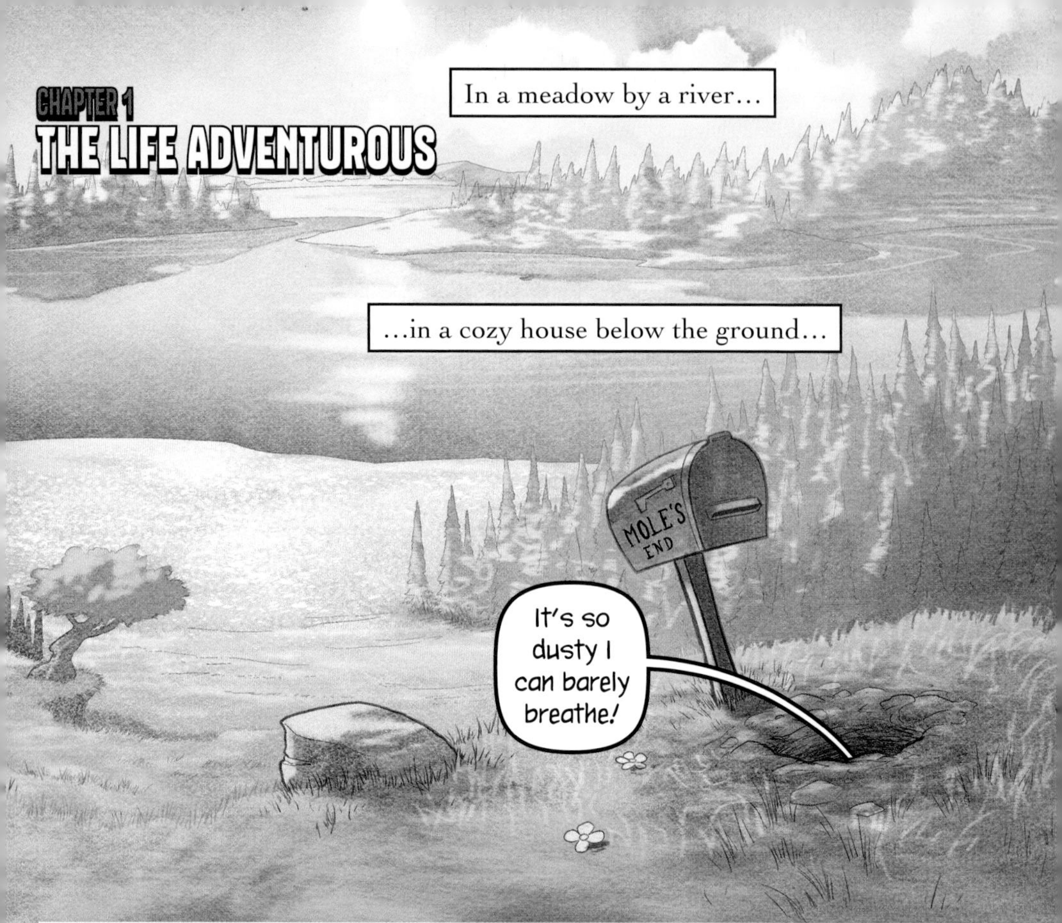
In a meadow by a river...
...in a cozy house below the ground...
MOLE'S END
It's so dusty I can barely breathe!

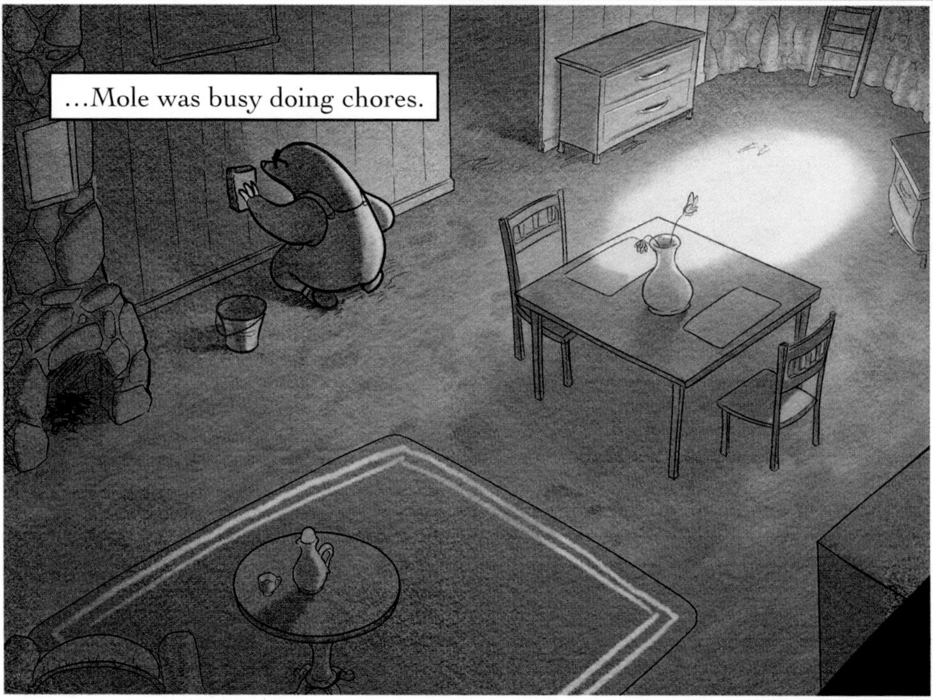
...Mole was busy doing chores.

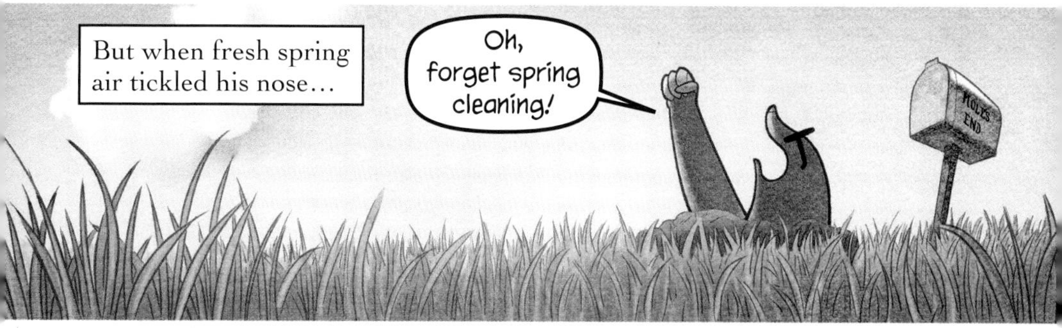
But when fresh spring air tickled his nose...
Oh, forget spring cleaning!
MOLE'S END

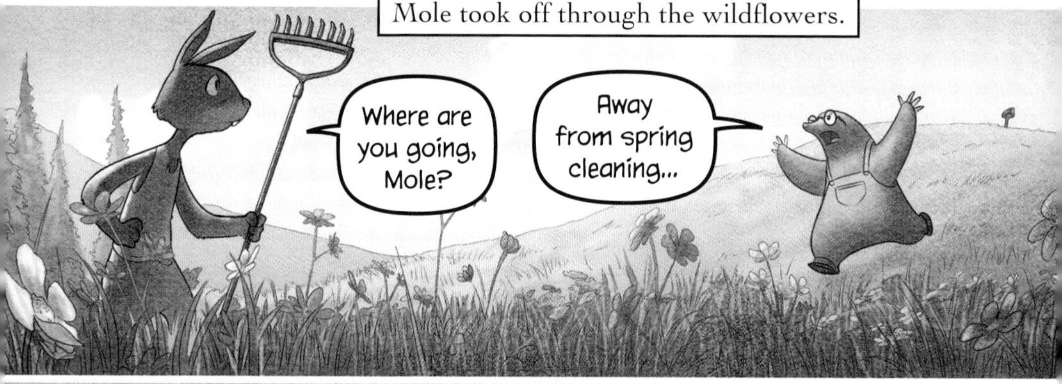
Mole took off through the wildflowers.
Where are you going, Mole?
Away from spring cleaning...

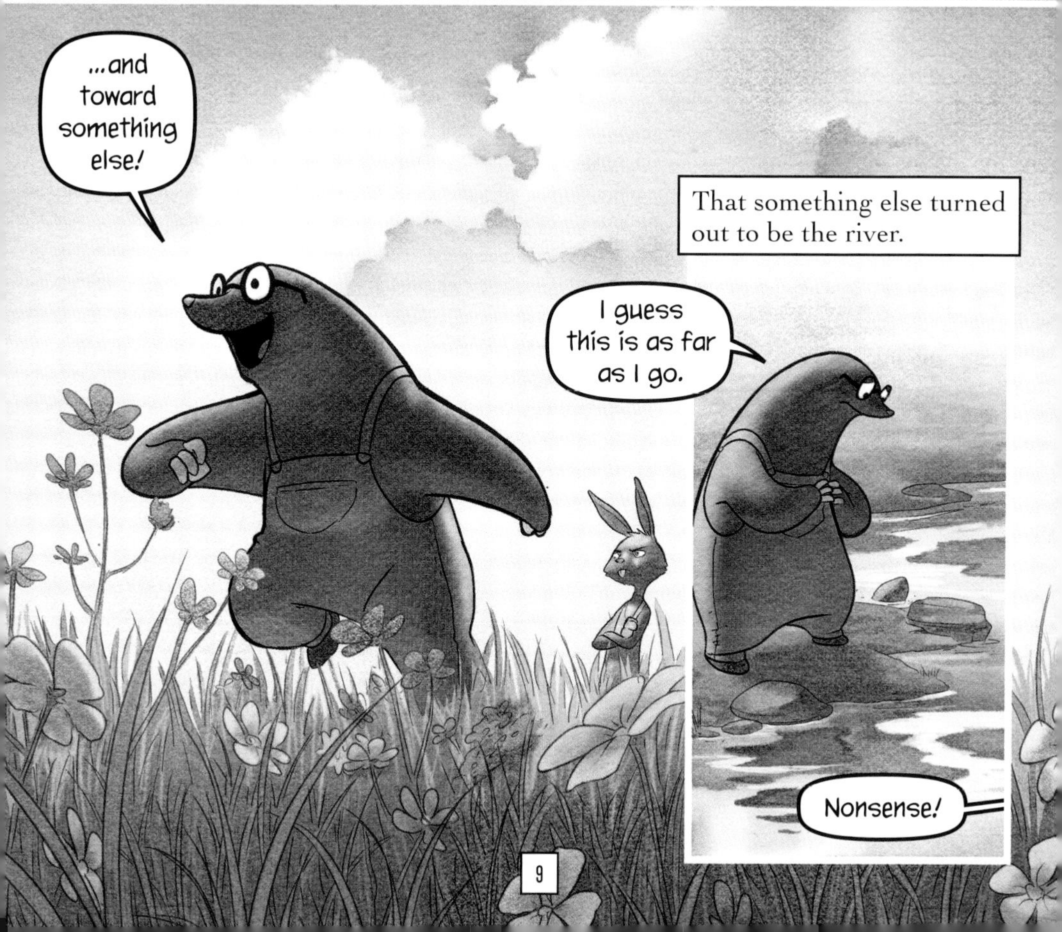
...and toward something else!
That something else turned out to be the river.
I guess this is as far as I go.
Nonsense!

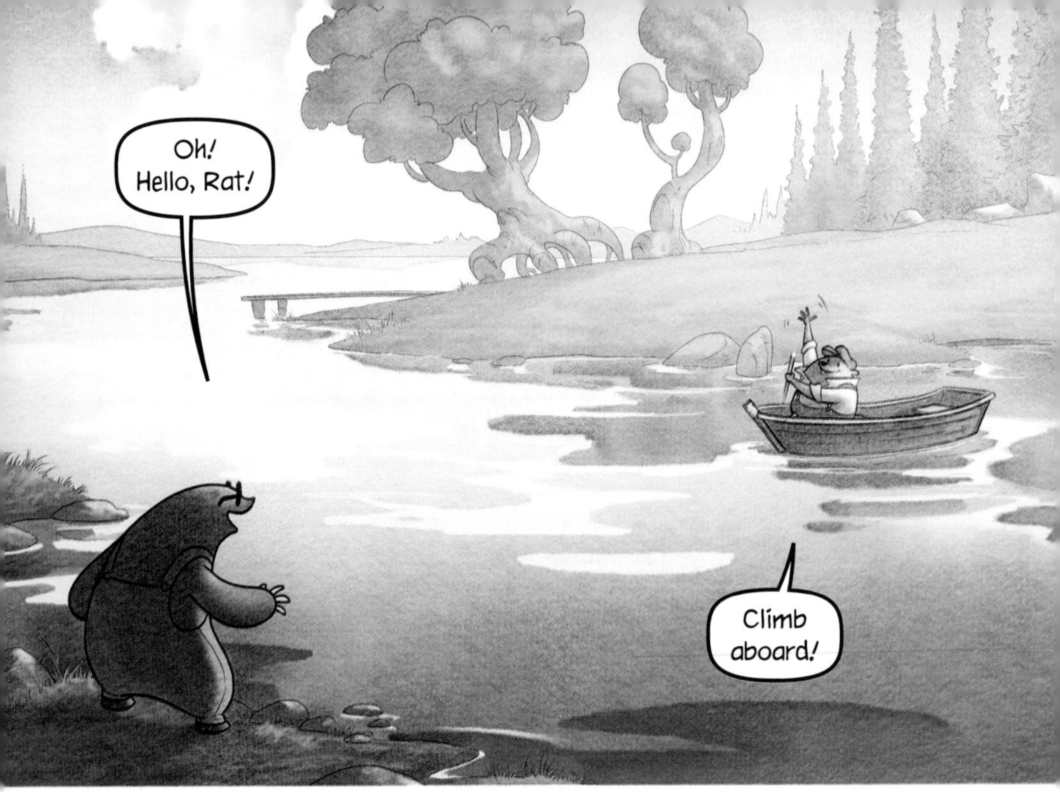
Oh! Hello, Rat!
Climb aboard!

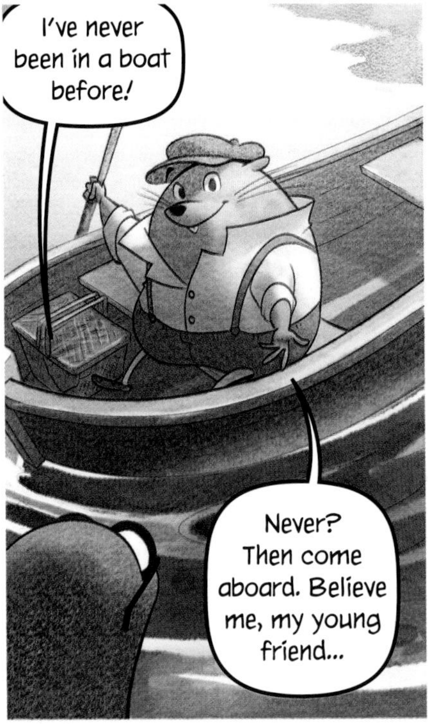
I've never been in a boat before!
Never? Then come aboard. Believe me, my young friend...

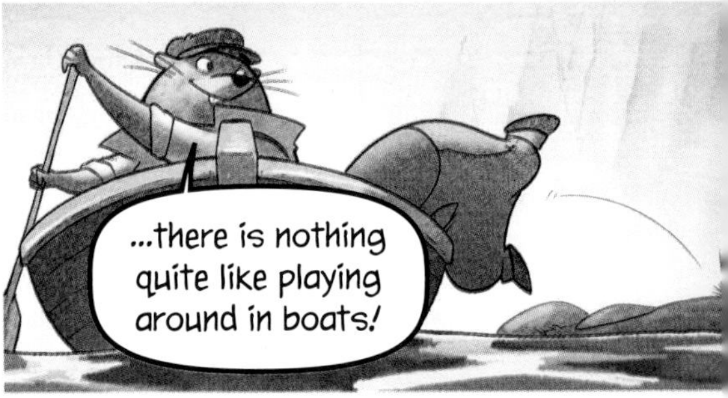
...there is nothing quite like playing around in boats!

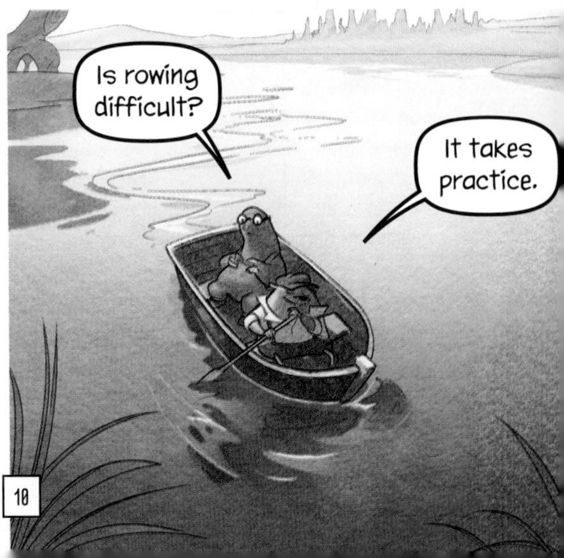
Is rowing difficult?
It takes practice.

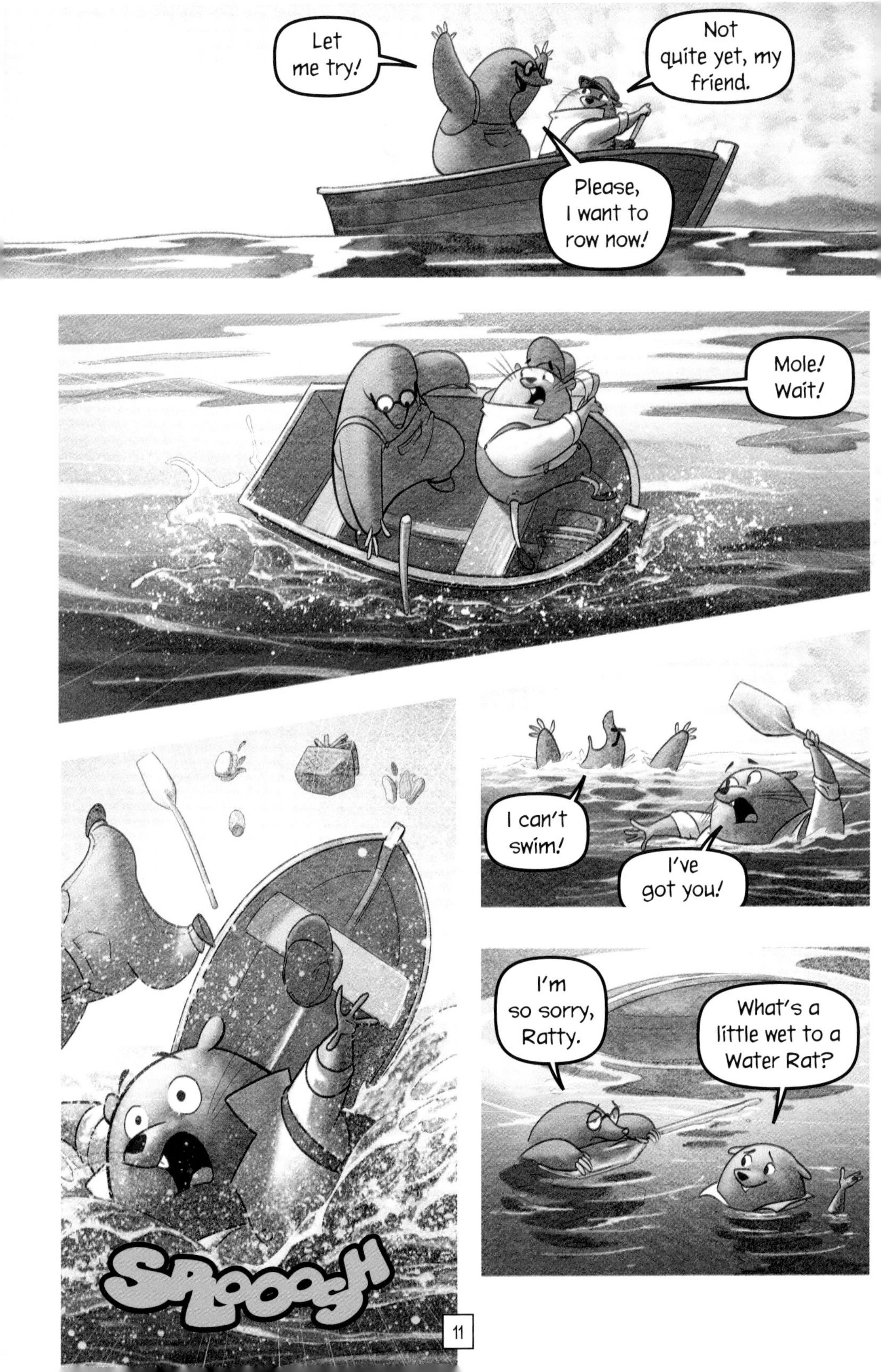
Let me try!
Not quite yet, my friend.
Please, I want to row now!
Mole! Wait!
SPLOOSH
I can't swim!
I've got you!
I'm so sorry, Ratty.
What's a little wet to a Water Rat?

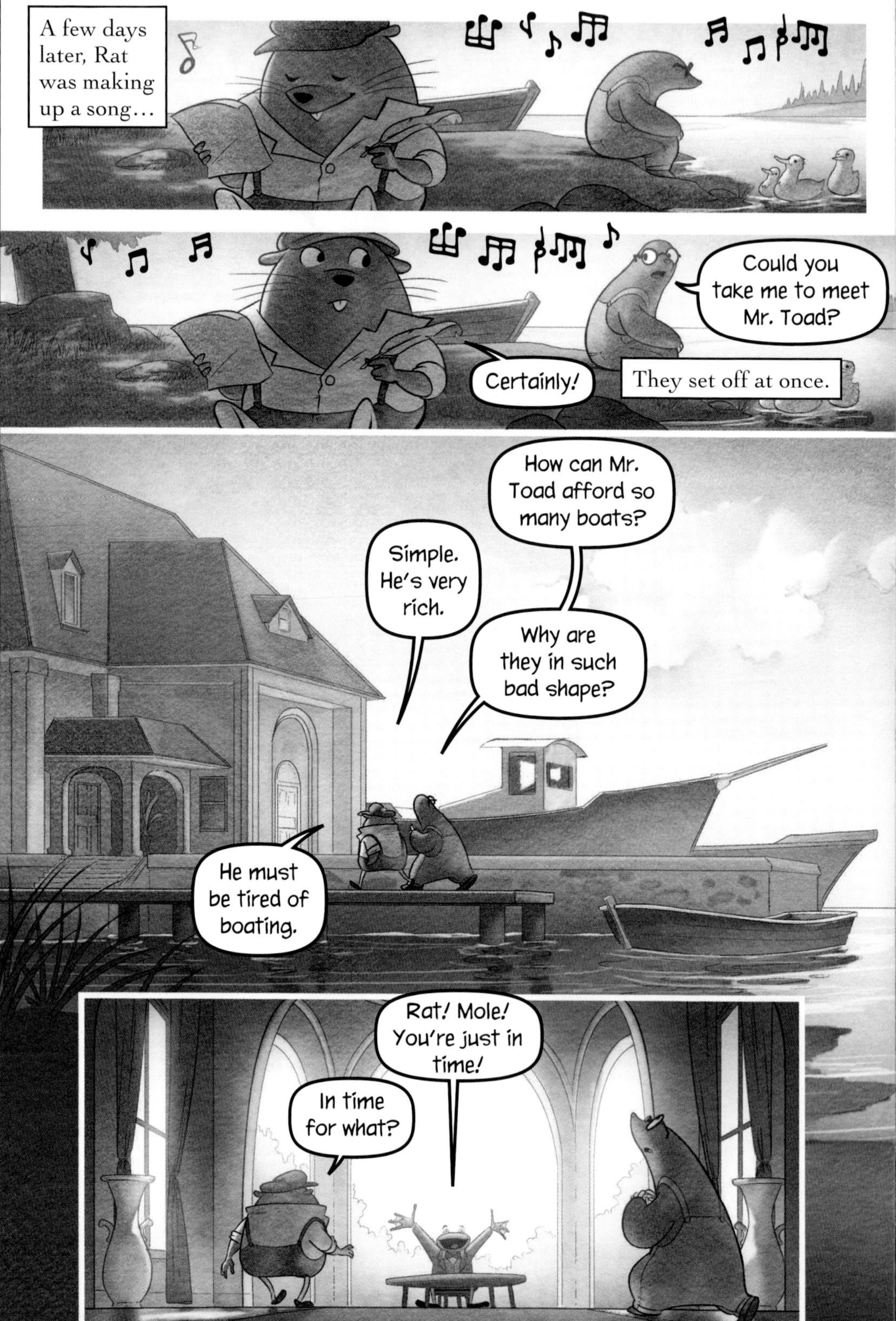
A few days later, Rat was making up a song…
Could you take me to meet Mr. Toad?
Certainly!
They set off at once.
How can Mr. Toad afford so many boats?
Simple. He's very rich.
Why are they in such bad shape?
He must be tired of boating.
Rat! Mole! You're just in time!
In time for what?

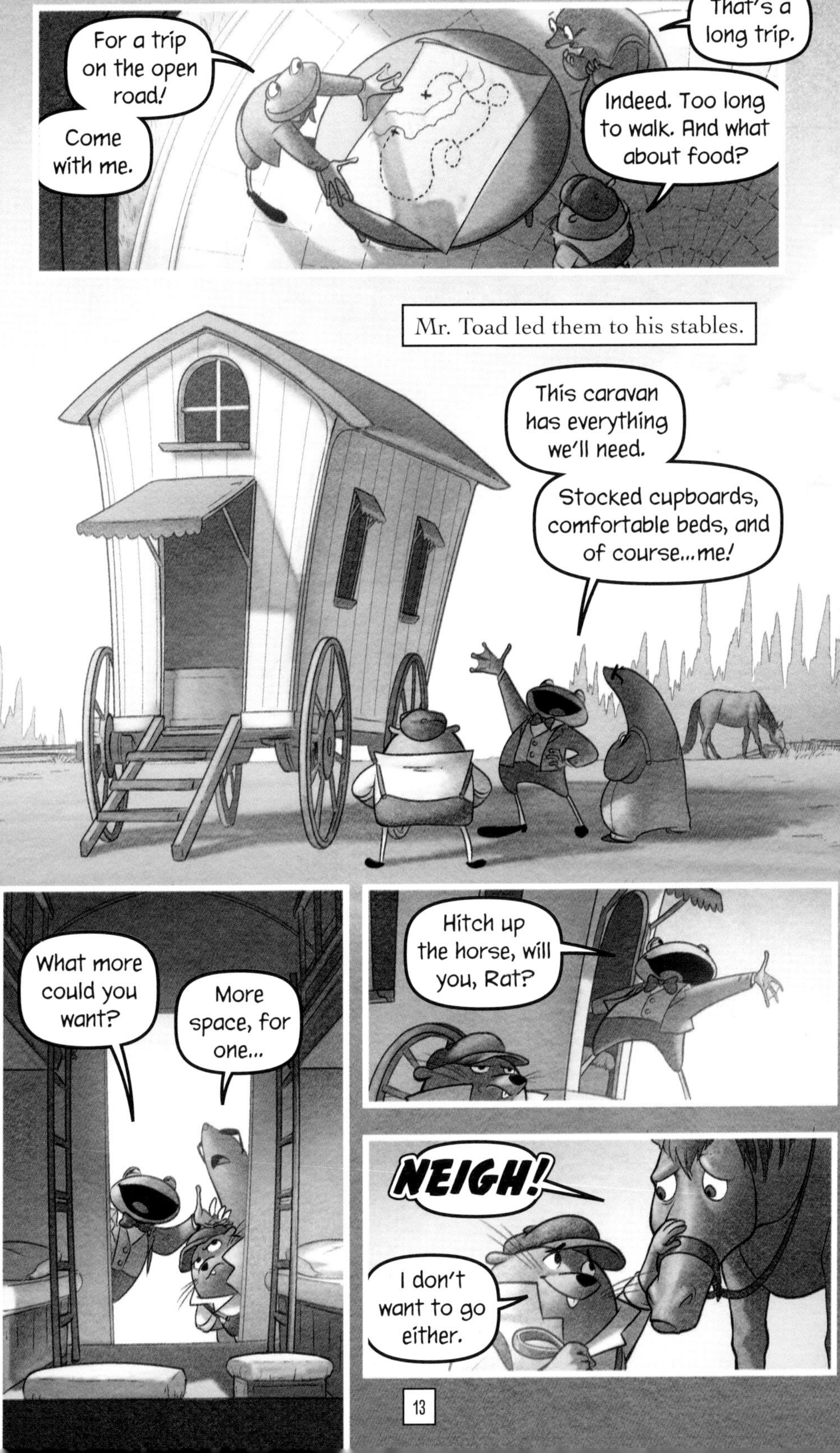
For a trip on the open road!
Come with me.
That's a long trip.
Indeed. Too long to walk. And what about food?
Mr. Toad led them to his stables.
This caravan has everything we'll need.
Stocked cupboards, comfortable beds, and of course...me!
What more could you want?
More space, for one...
Hitch up the horse, will you, Rat?
NEIGH!
I don't want to go either.

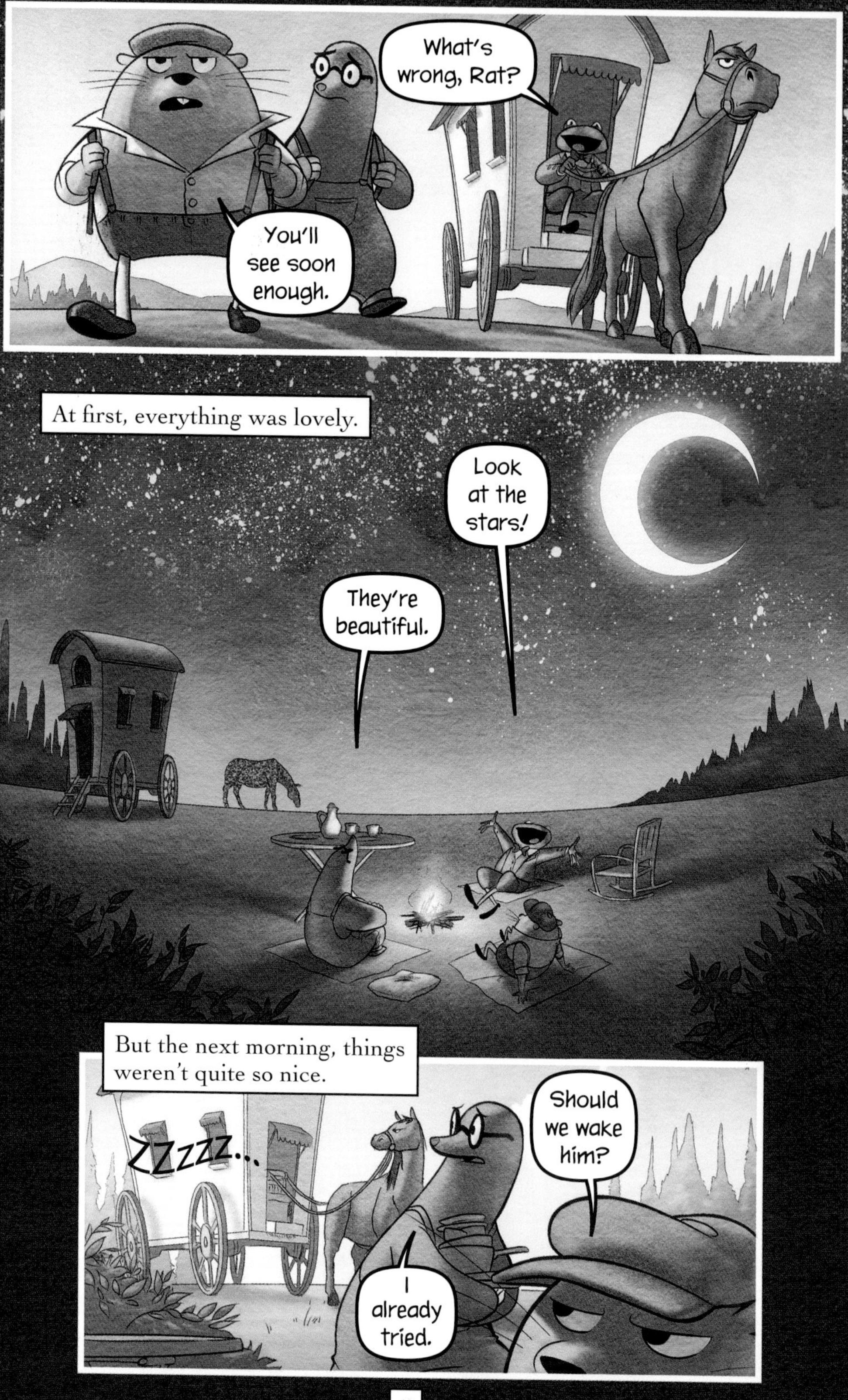
What's wrong, Rat?
You'll see soon enough.
At first, everything was lovely.
Look at the stars!
They're beautiful.
But the next morning, things weren't quite so nice.
ZZzzz...
Should we wake him?
I already tried.

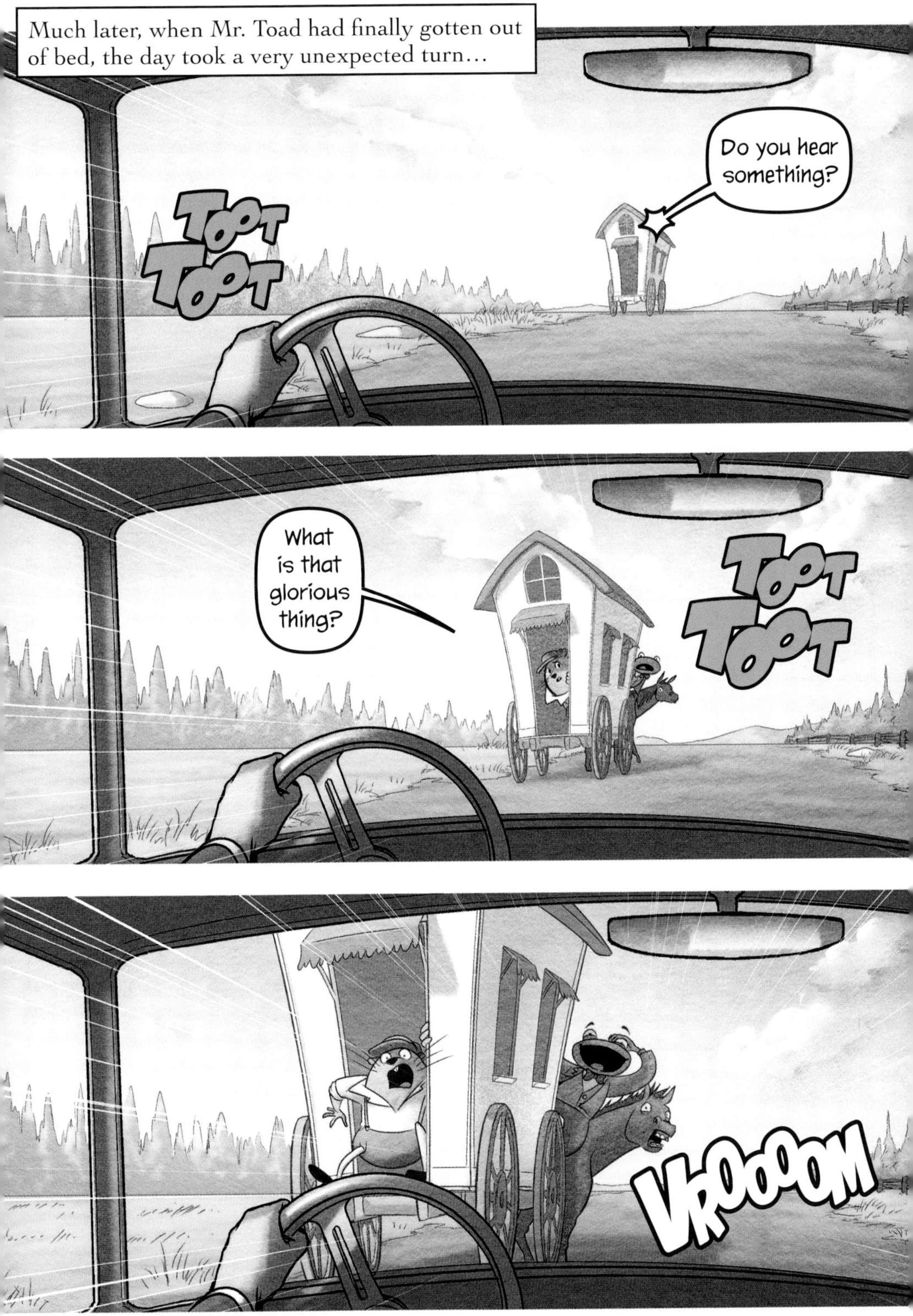
Much later, when Mr. Toad had finally gotten out of bed, the day took a very unexpected turn…
TOOT TOOT
Do you hear something?
What is that glorious thing?
TOOT TOOT
VROOOOM

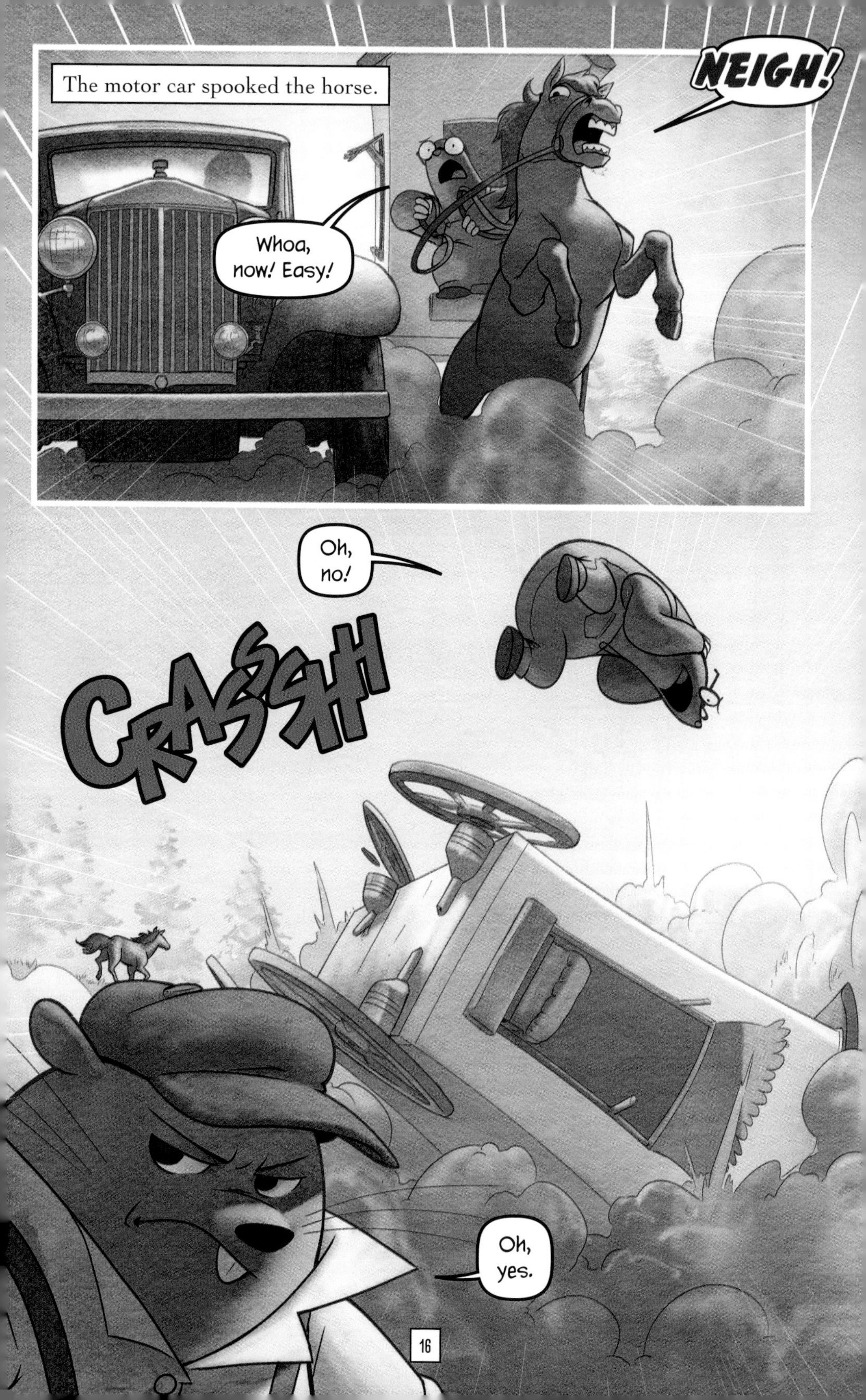

The motor car spooked the horse.
Whoa, now! Easy!
NEIGH!
Oh, no!
CRASSHH
Oh, yes.

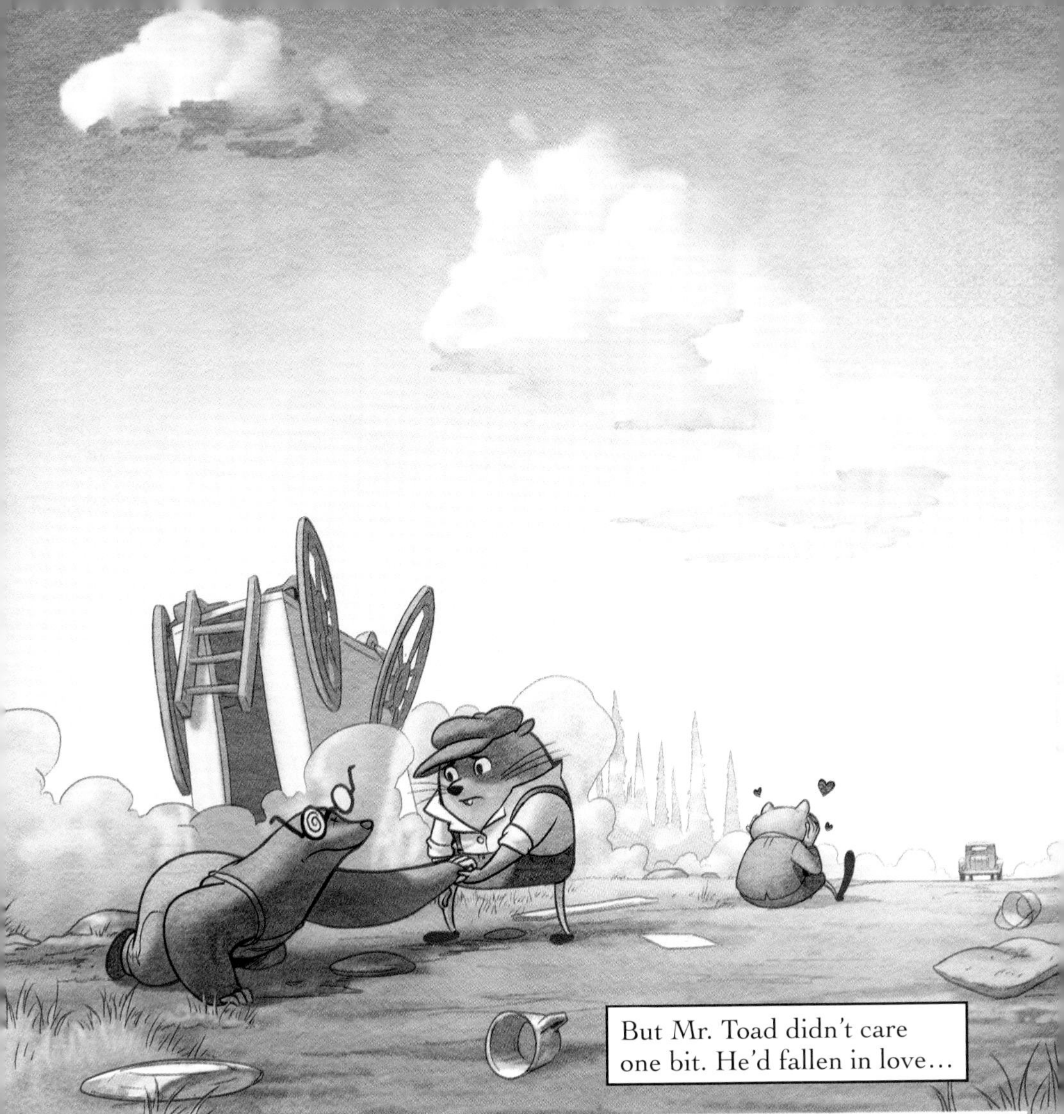
But Mr. Toad didn't care one bit. He'd fallen in love…

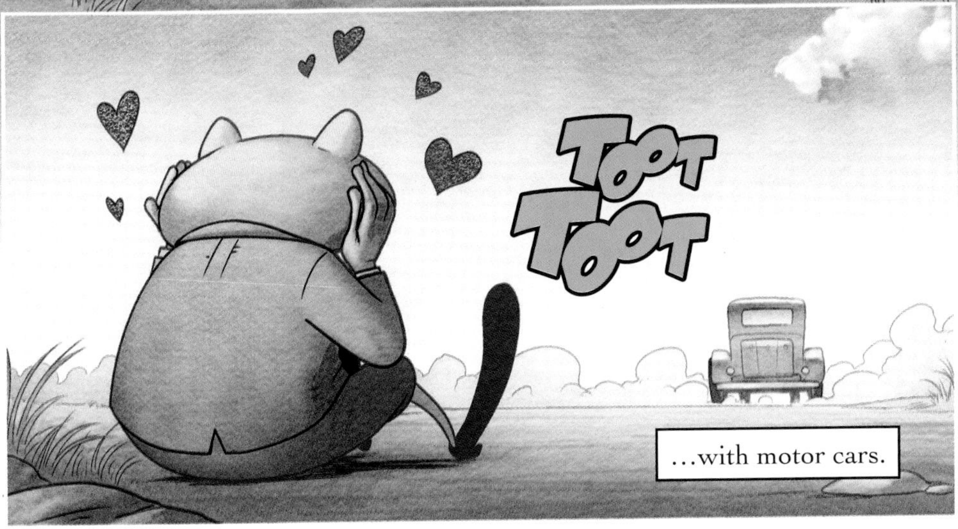
TOOT
TOOT
…with motor cars.

CHAPTER 2
DANGER IN THE WILD WOOD

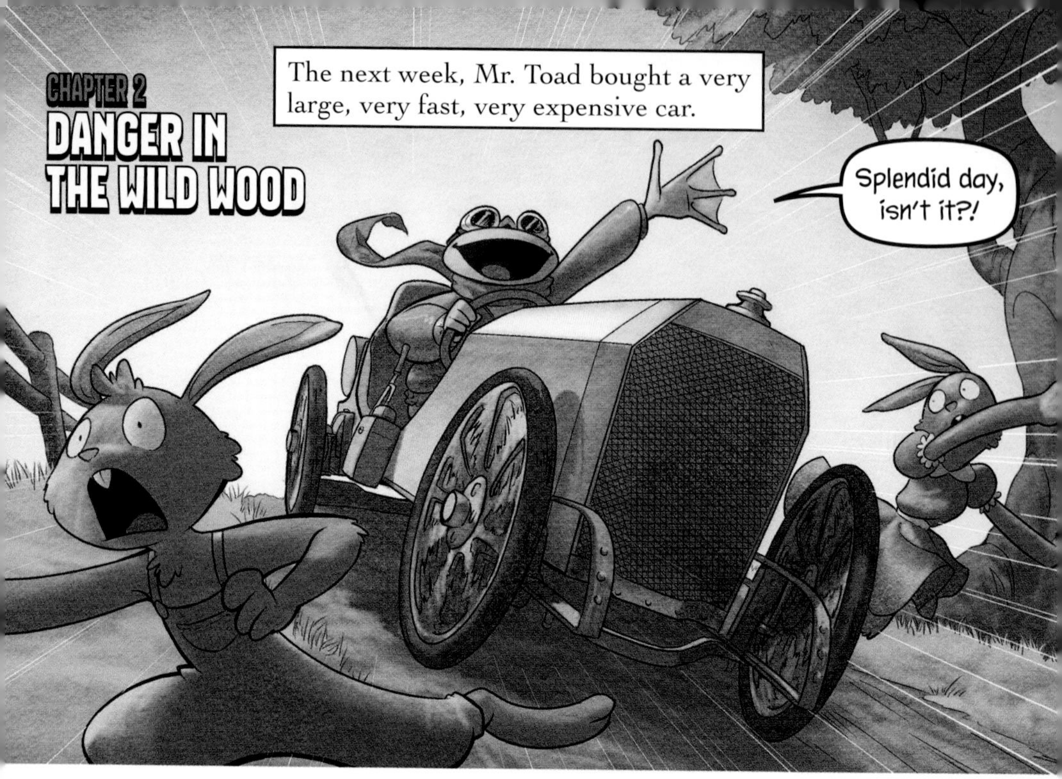
The next week, Mr. Toad bought a very large, very fast, very expensive car.
Splendid day, isn't it?!

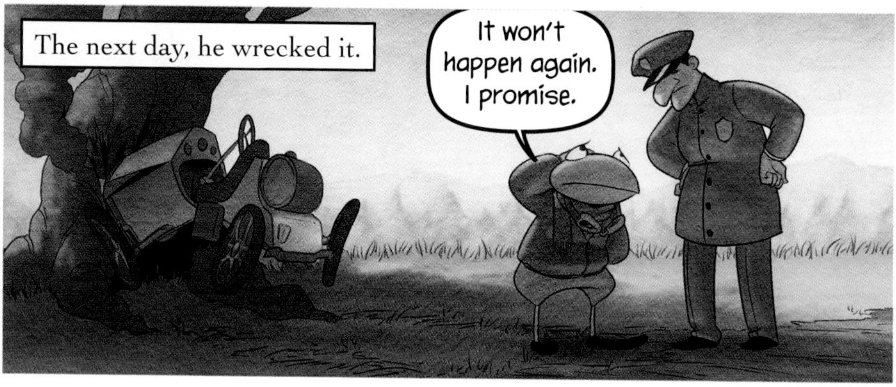
The next day, he wrecked it.
It won't happen again. I promise.

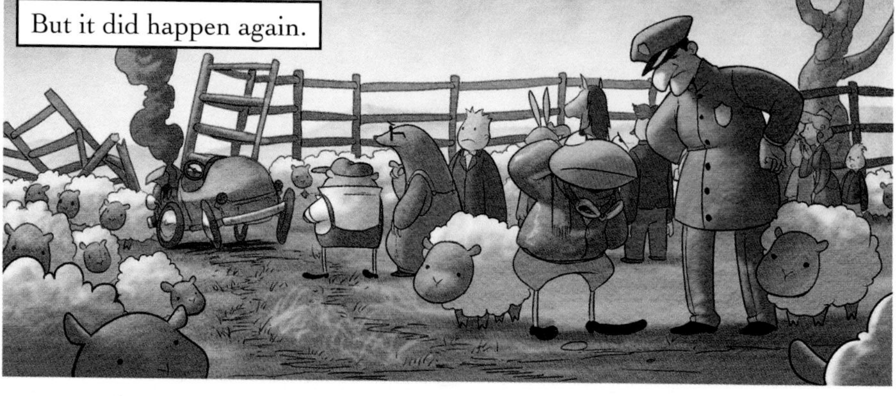
But it did happen again.

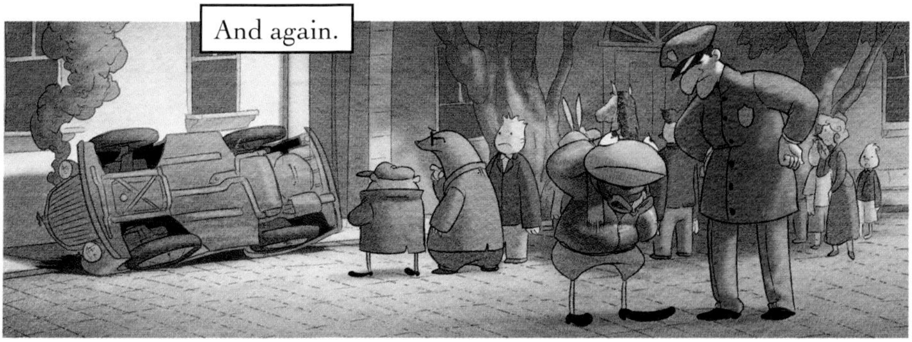
And again.

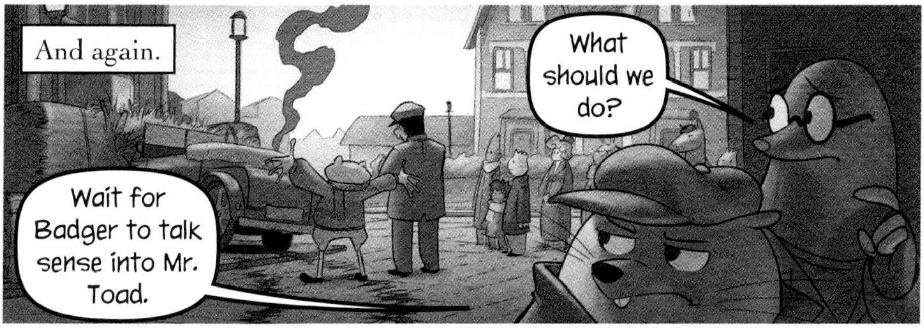
And again.
What should we do?
Wait for Badger to talk sense into Mr. Toad.

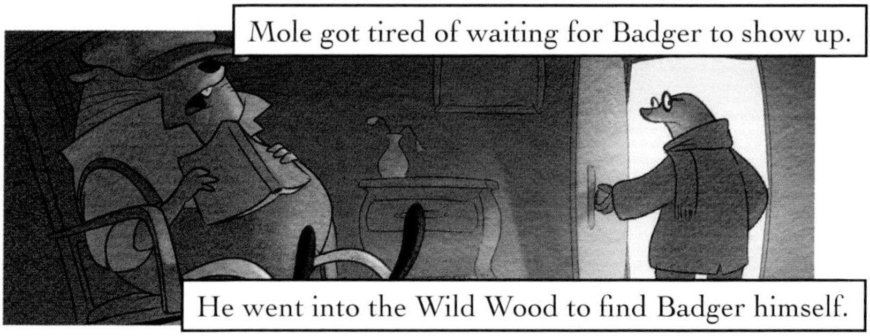
Mole got tired of waiting for Badger to show up.
He went into the Wild Wood to find Badger himself.

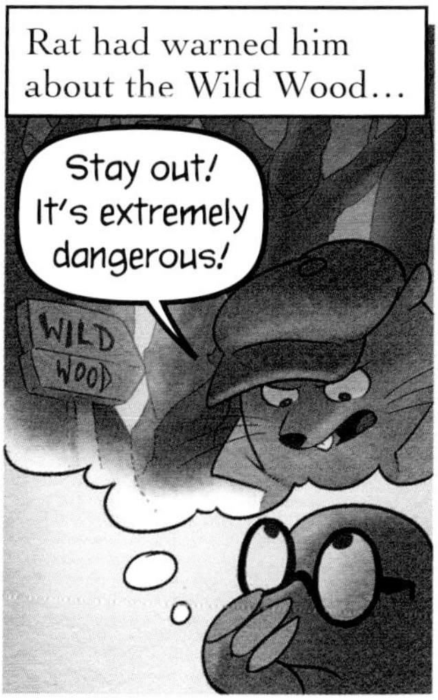
Rat had warned him about the Wild Wood...
Stay out! It's extremely dangerous!
WILD WOOD

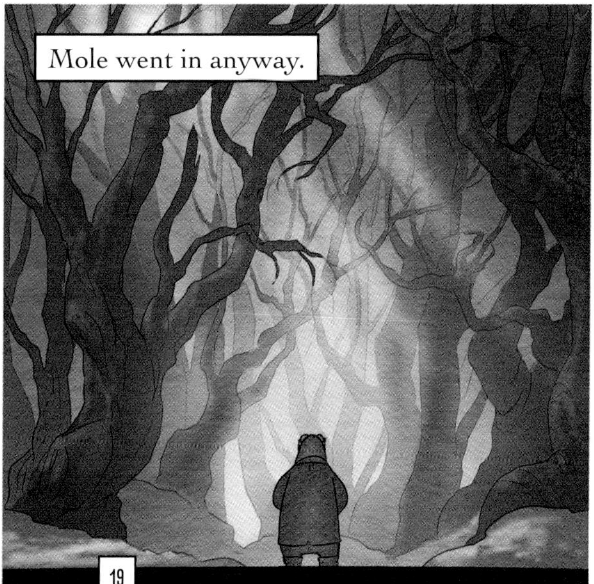
Mole went in anyway.

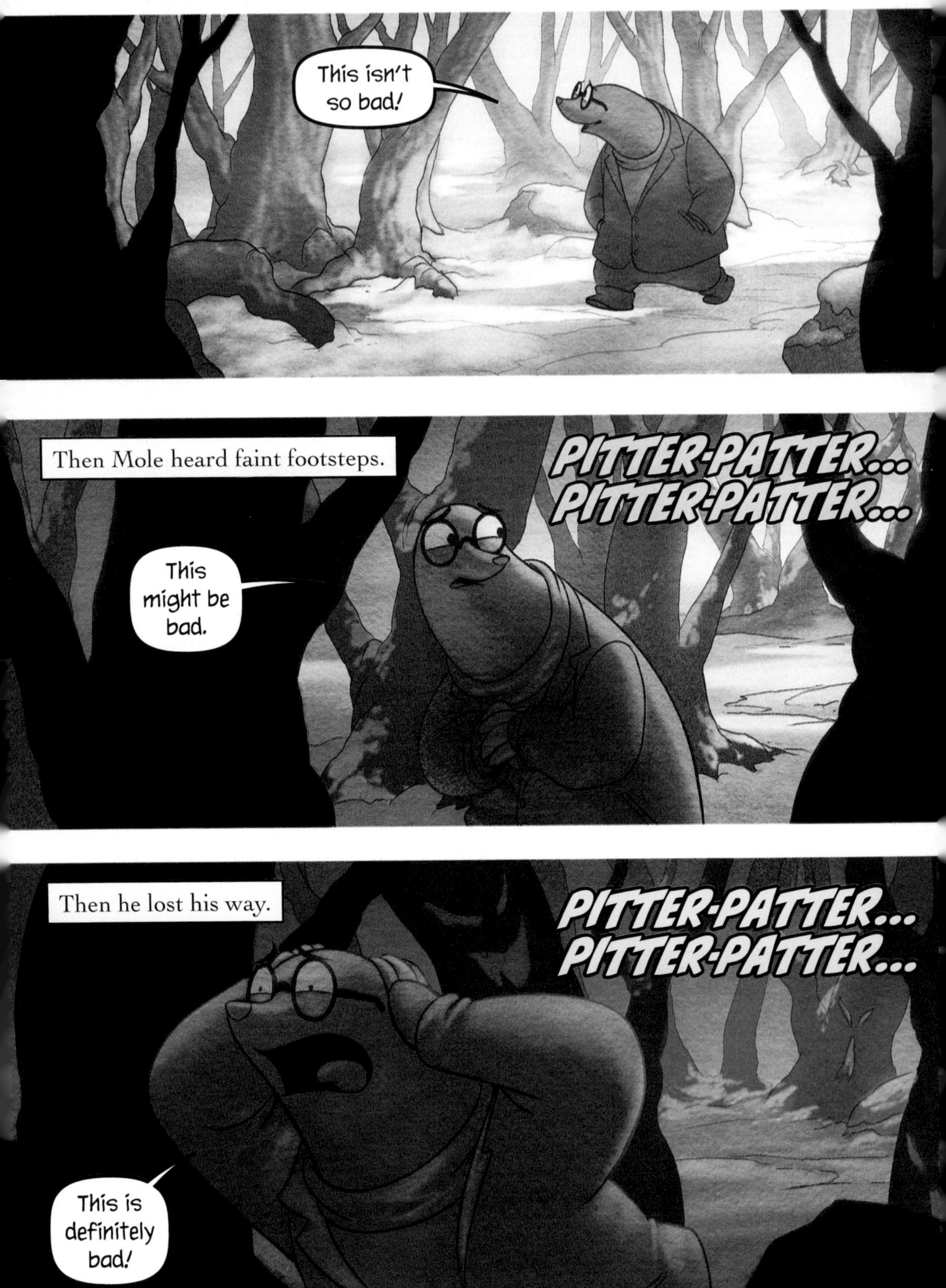
This isn't so bad!
Then Mole heard faint footsteps.
PITTER-PATTER... PITTER-PATTER...
This might be bad.
Then he lost his way.
PITTER-PATTER... PITTER-PATTER...
This is definitely bad!

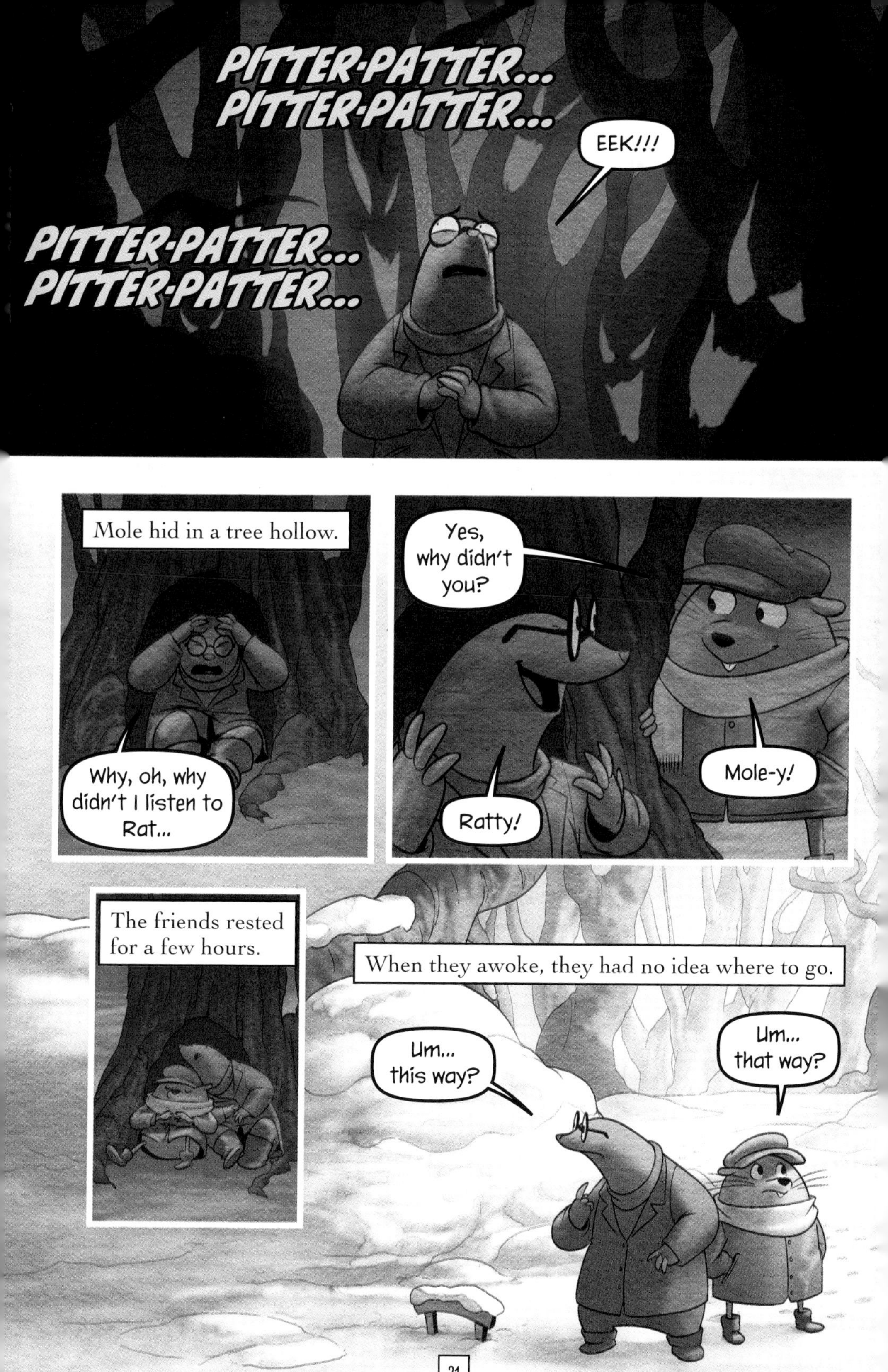
PITTER-PATTER...
PITTER-PATTER...
EEK!!!
PITTER-PATTER...
PITTER-PATTER...
Mole hid in a tree hollow.
Why, oh, why didn't I listen to Rat...
Yes, why didn't you?
Ratty!
Mole-y!
The friends rested for a few hours.
When they awoke, they had no idea where to go.
Um... this way?
Um... that way?

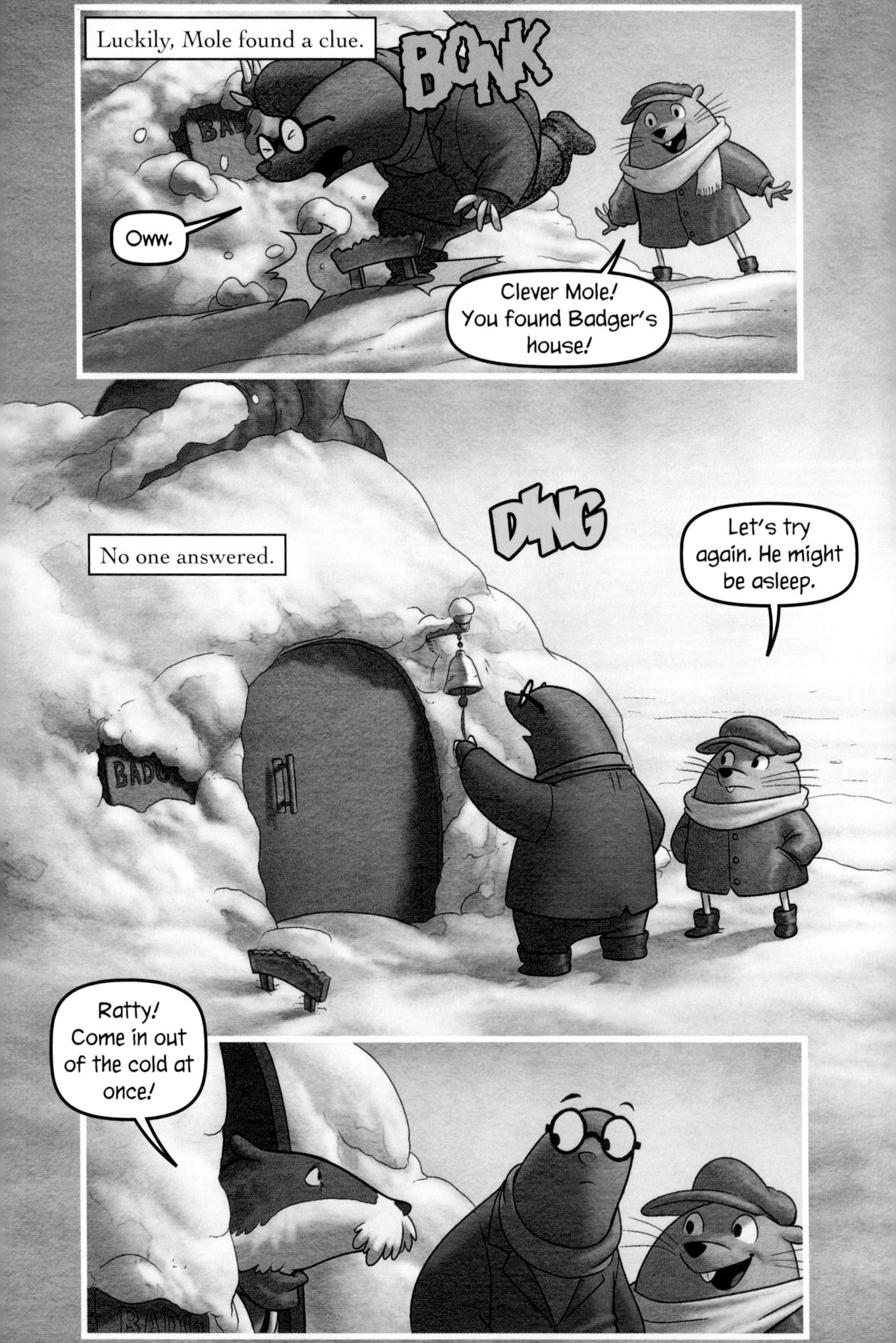
Luckily, Mole found a clue.
BONK
Oww.
Clever Mole! You found Badger's house!
DING
No one answered.
Let's try again. He might be asleep.
Ratty! Come in out of the cold at once!

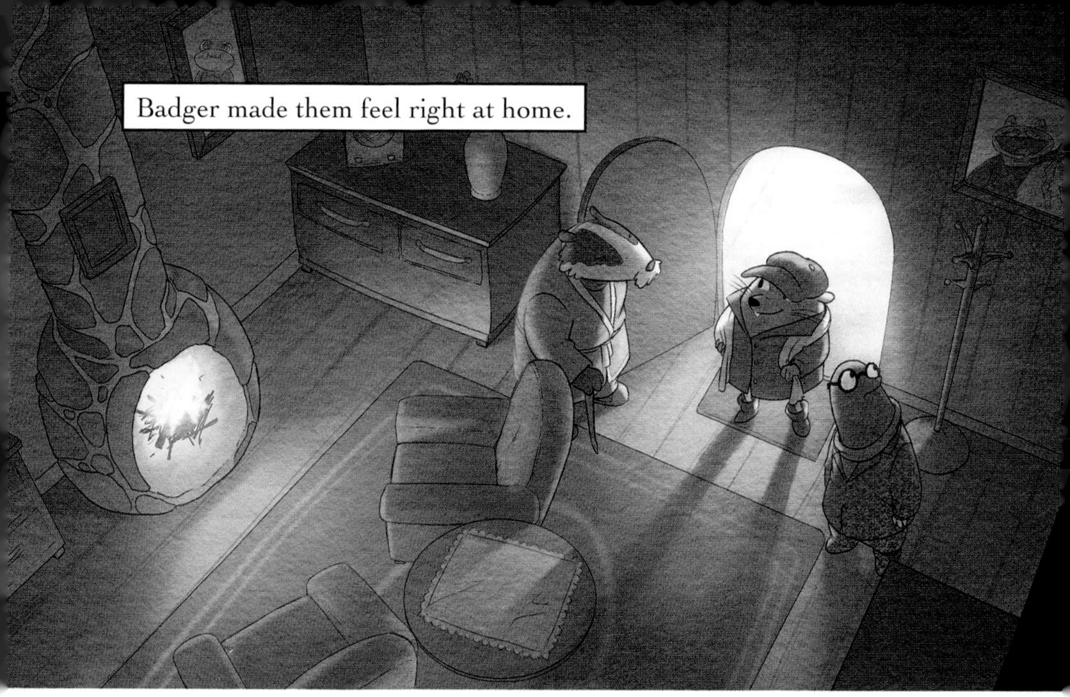
Badger made them feel right at home.

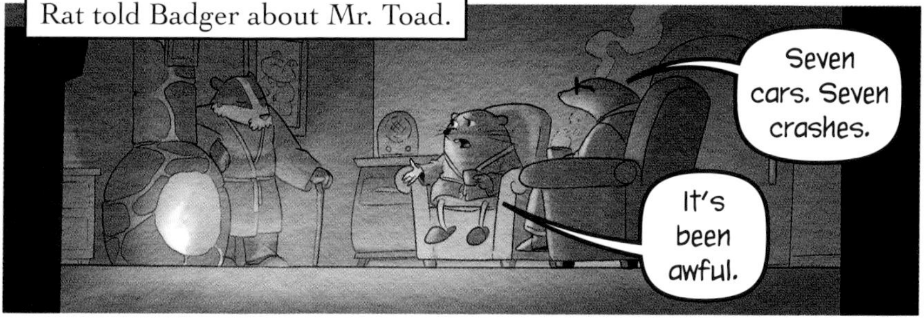
Rat told Badger about Mr. Toad.
Seven cars. Seven crashes.
It's been awful.

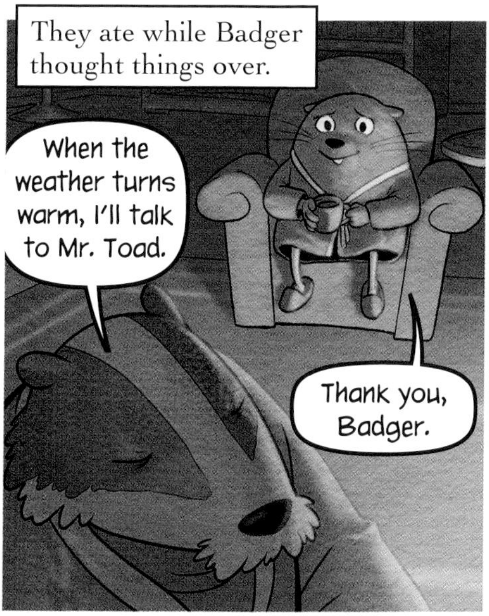
They ate while Badger thought things over.
When the weather turns warm, I'll talk to Mr. Toad.
Thank you, Badger.

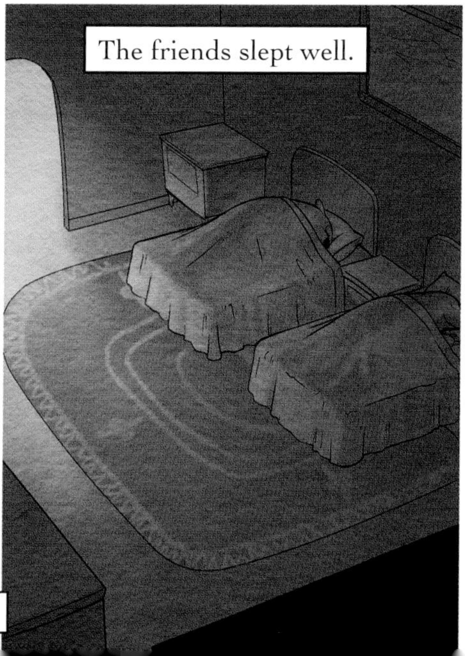
The friends slept well.

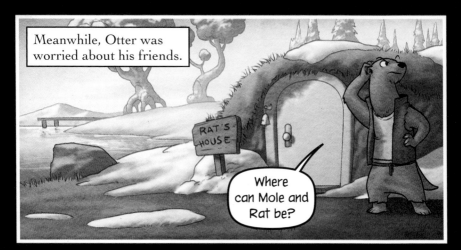

Meanwhile, Otter was worried about his friends.

RAT'S HOUSE

Where can Mole and Rat be?

The next morning, Otter tracked them down.

Found you!

Haha! Get off!

Otter, weren't you scared? Being all alone in Wild Wood?

No one would dare try anything with me!

Luckily, Badger had built a secret passage back to the river.

This way!

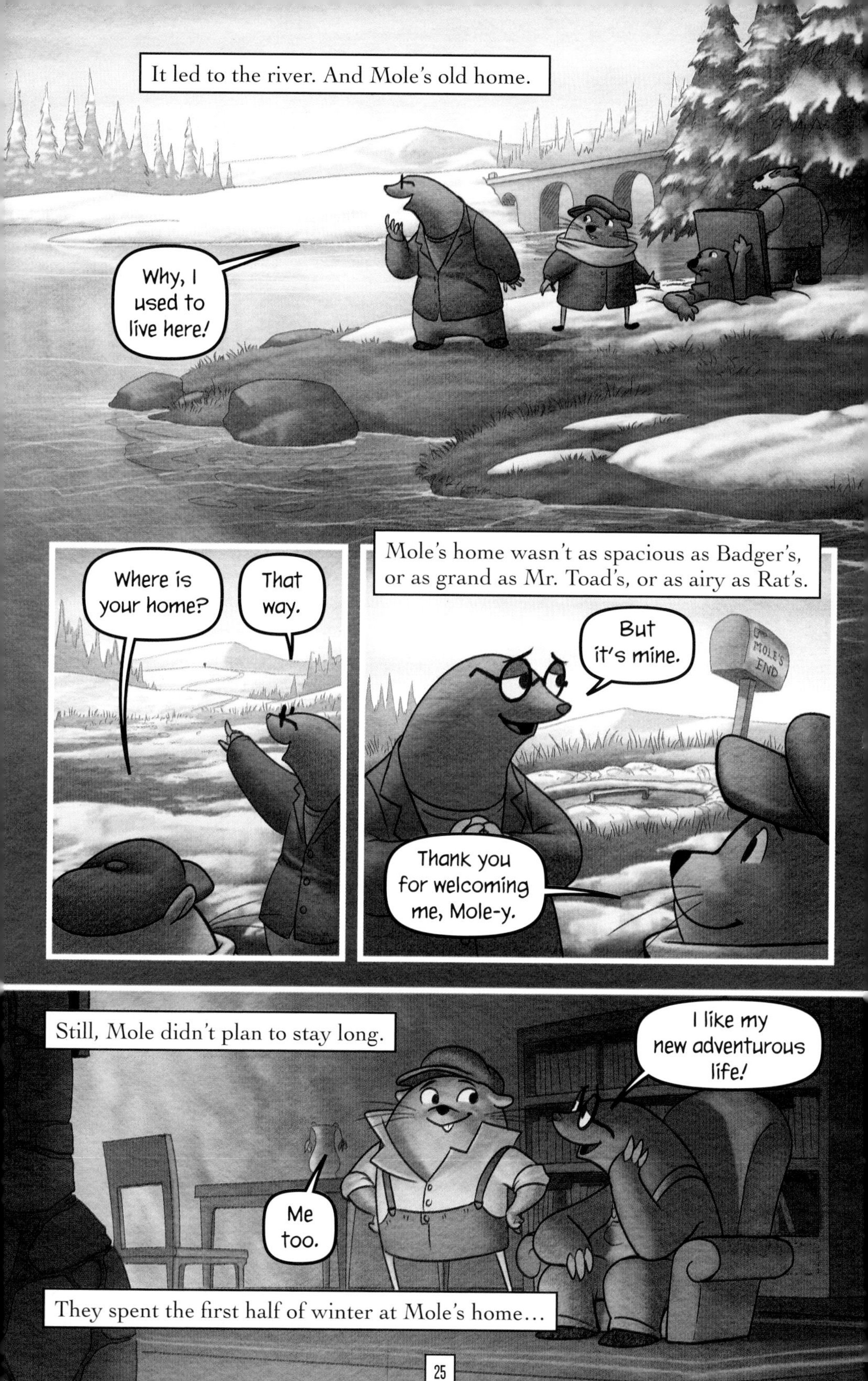
It led to the river. And Mole's old home.
Why, I used to live here!
Where is your home?
That way.
Mole's home wasn't as spacious as Badger's, or as grand as Mr. Toad's, or as airy as Rat's.
But it's mine.
MOLE'S END
Thank you for welcoming me, Mole-y.
Still, Mole didn't plan to stay long.
I like my new adventurous life!
Me too.
They spent the first half of winter at Mole's home…

CHAPTER 3
MR. TOAD'S FOLLY

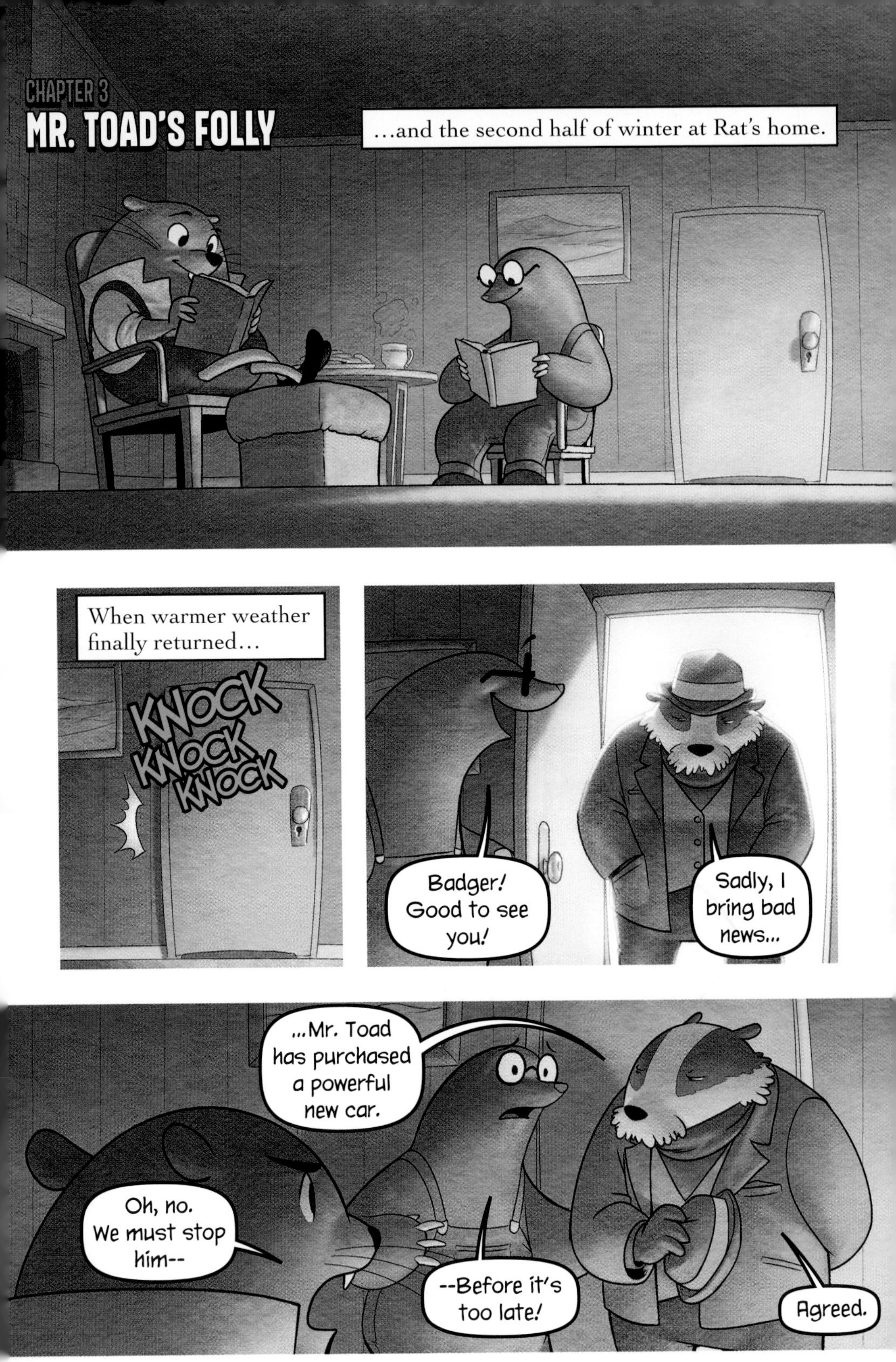

...and the second half of winter at Rat's home.
When warmer weather finally returned...
KNOCK KNOCK KNOCK
Badger! Good to see you!
Sadly, I bring bad news...
...Mr. Toad has purchased a powerful new car.
Oh, no. We must stop him--
--Before it's too late!
Agreed.

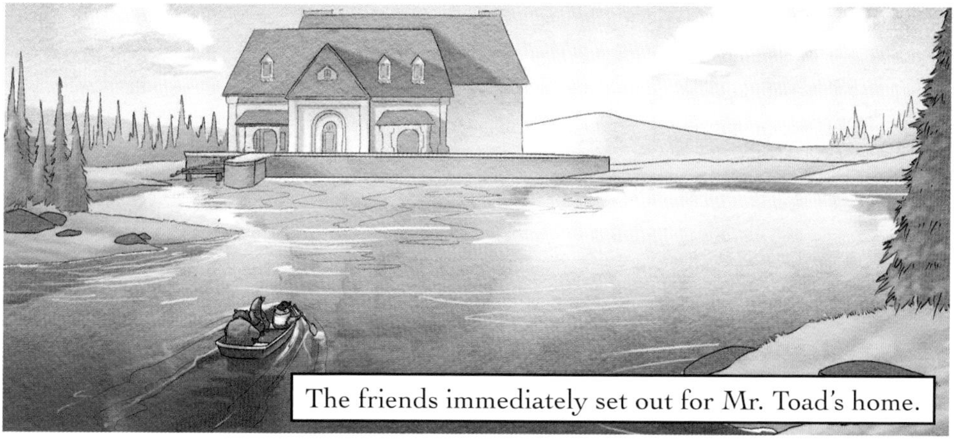
The friends immediately set out for Mr. Toad's home.

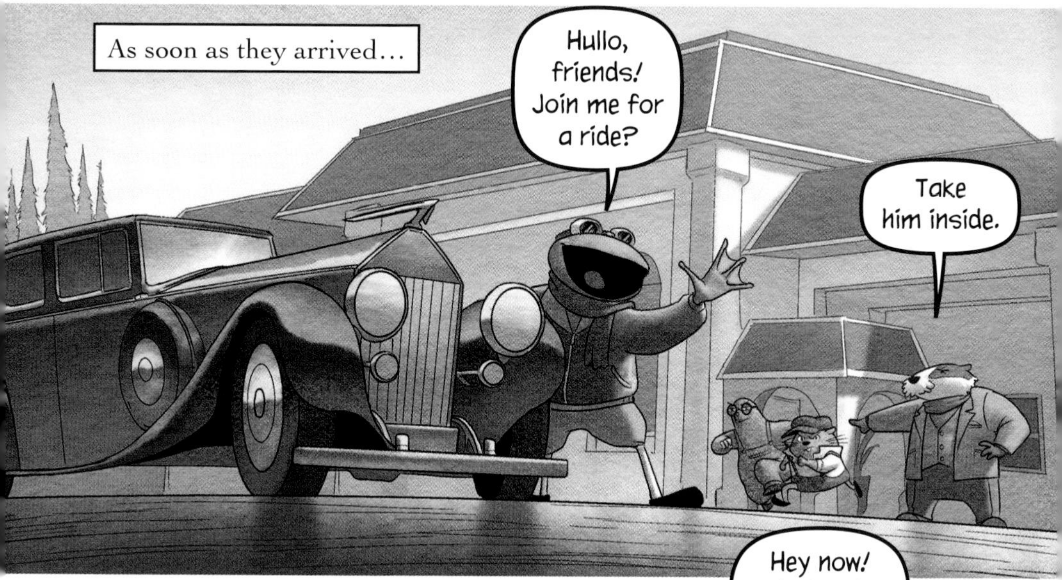
As soon as they arrived…
Hullo, friends! Join me for a ride?
Take him inside.

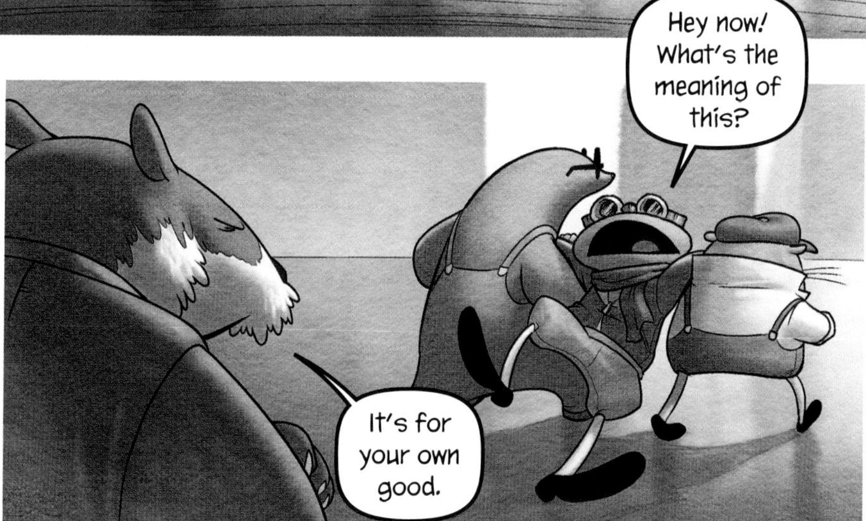
Hey now! What's the meaning of this?
It's for your own good.

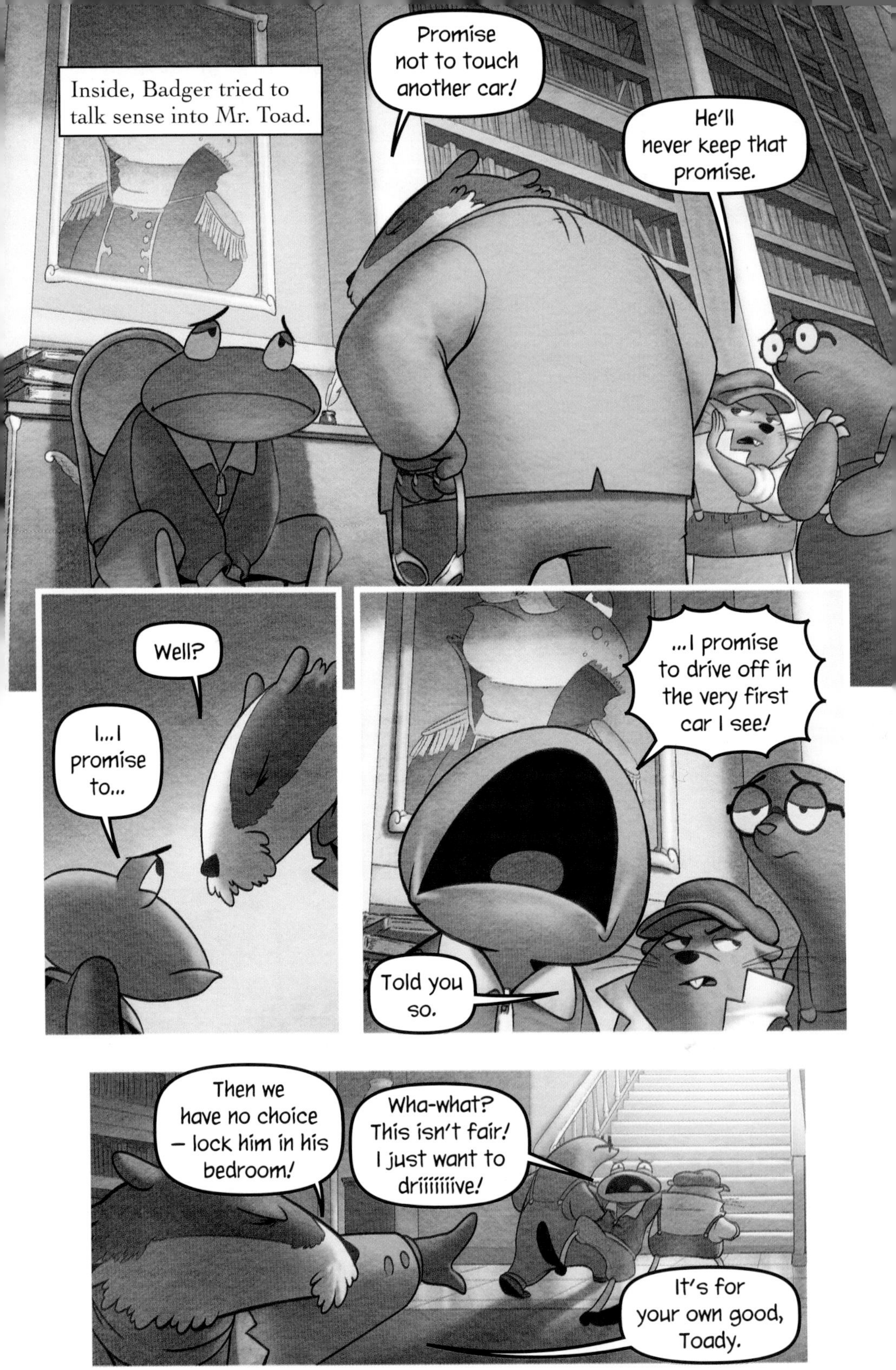
Inside, Badger tried to talk sense into Mr. Toad.
Promise not to touch another car!
He'll never keep that promise.
Well?
I...I promise to...
...I promise to drive off in the very first car I see!
Told you so.
Then we have no choice – lock him in his bedroom!
Wha-what? This isn't fair! I just want to driiiiiiive!
It's for your own good, Toady.

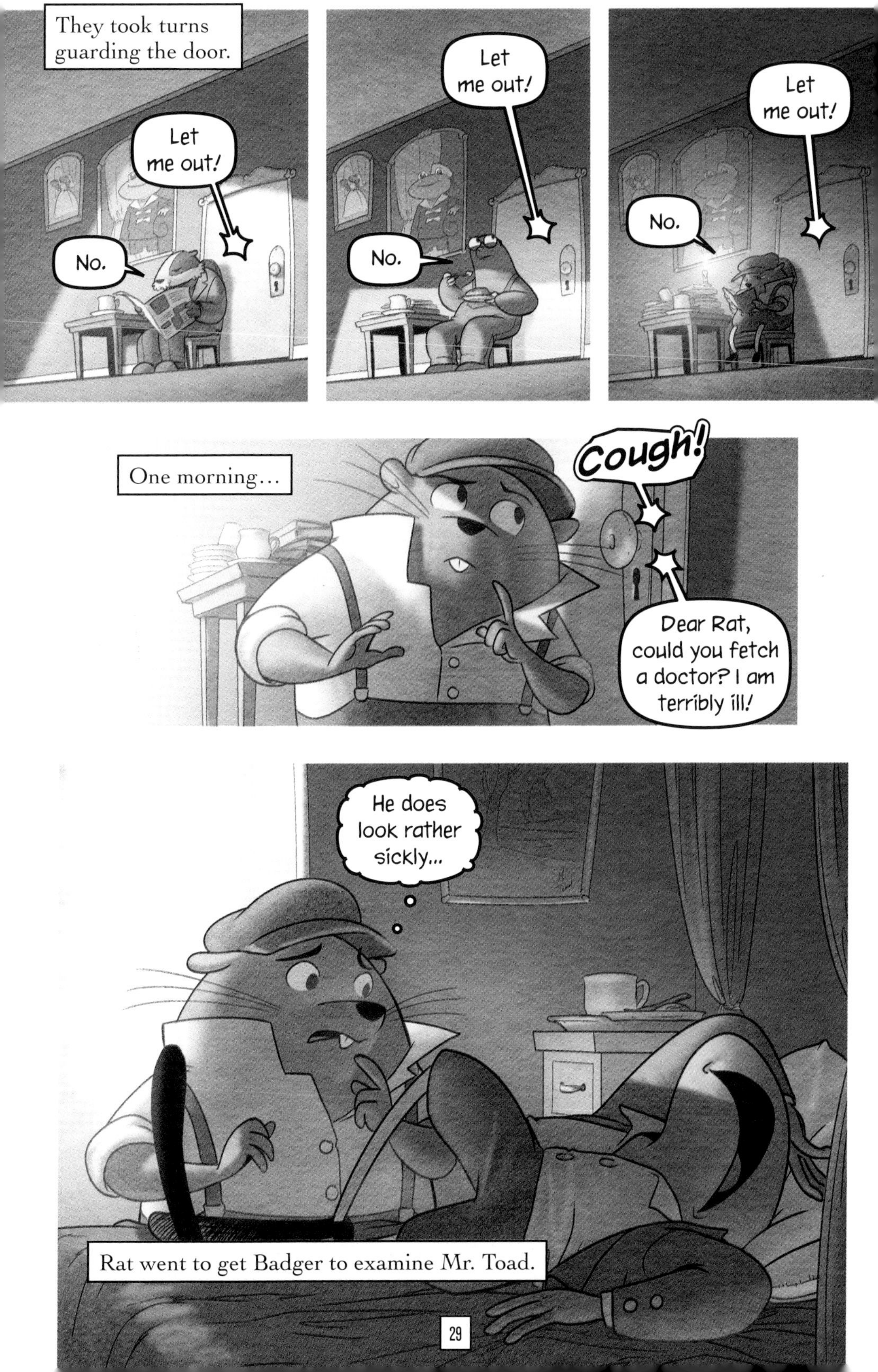
They took turns guarding the door.
Let me out!
No.
Let me out!
No.
Let me out!
No.
One morning…
Cough!
Dear Rat, could you fetch a doctor? I am terribly ill!
He does look rather sickly…
Rat went to get Badger to examine Mr. Toad.

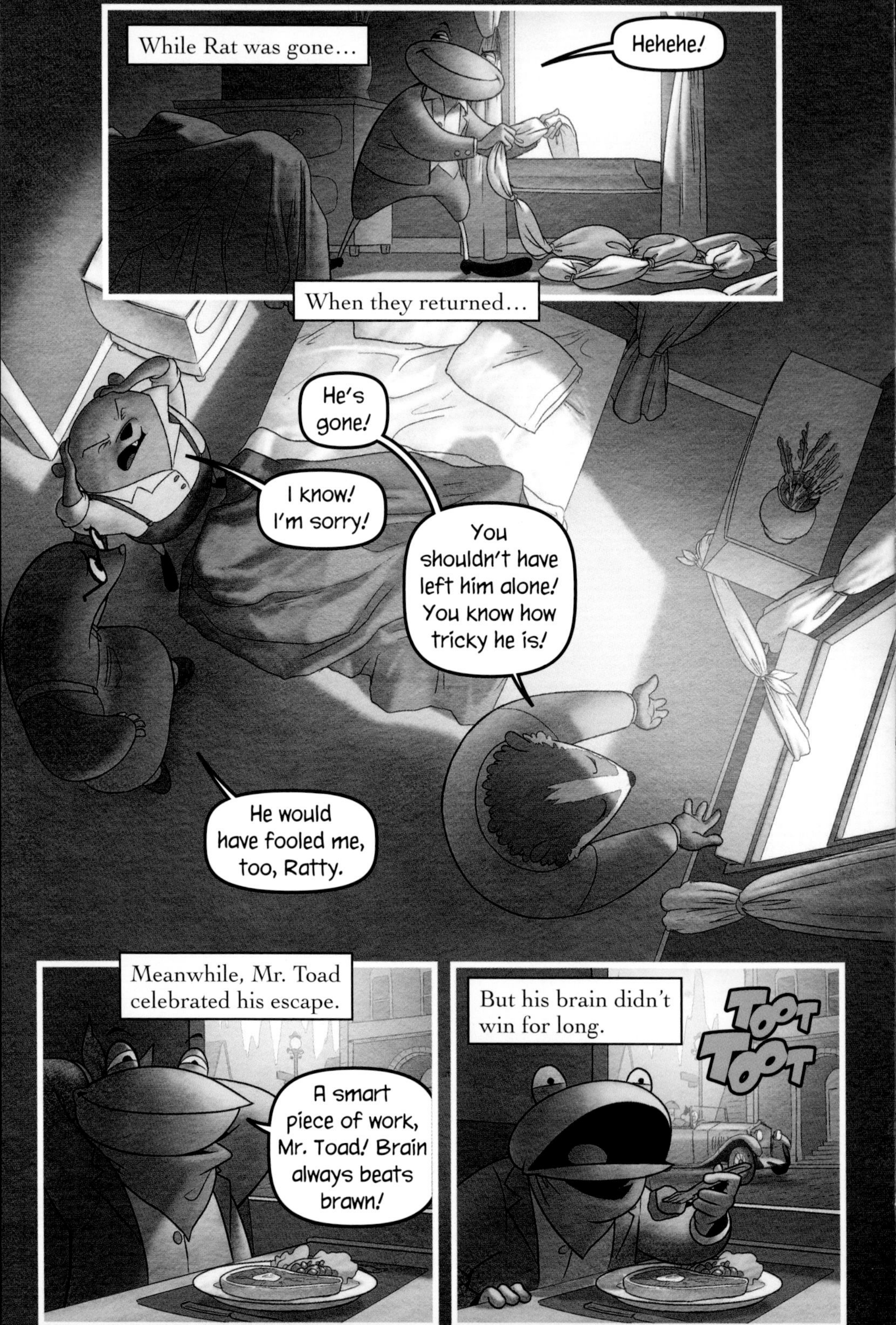

While Rat was gone…
Hehehe!
When they returned…
He's gone!
I know! I'm sorry!
You shouldn't have left him alone! You know how tricky he is!
He would have fooled me, too, Ratty.
Meanwhile, Mr. Toad celebrated his escape.
A smart piece of work, Mr. Toad! Brain always beats brawn!
But his brain didn't win for long.
TOOT TOOT

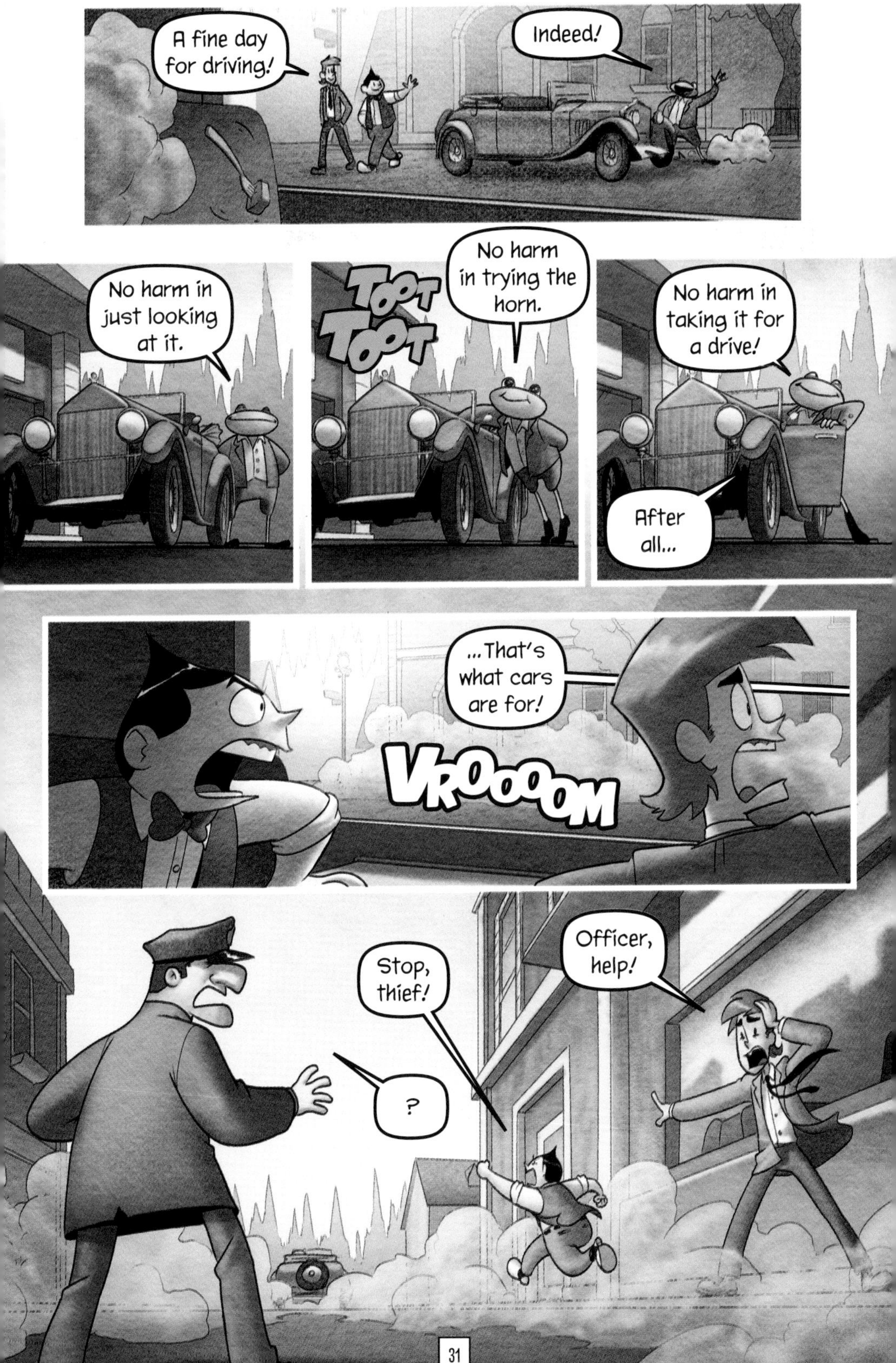

A fine day for driving!
Indeed!
No harm in just looking at it.
TOOT TOOT
No harm in trying the horn.
No harm in taking it for a drive!
After all...
...That's what cars are for!
VROOOOOM
Stop, thief!
Officer, help!
?

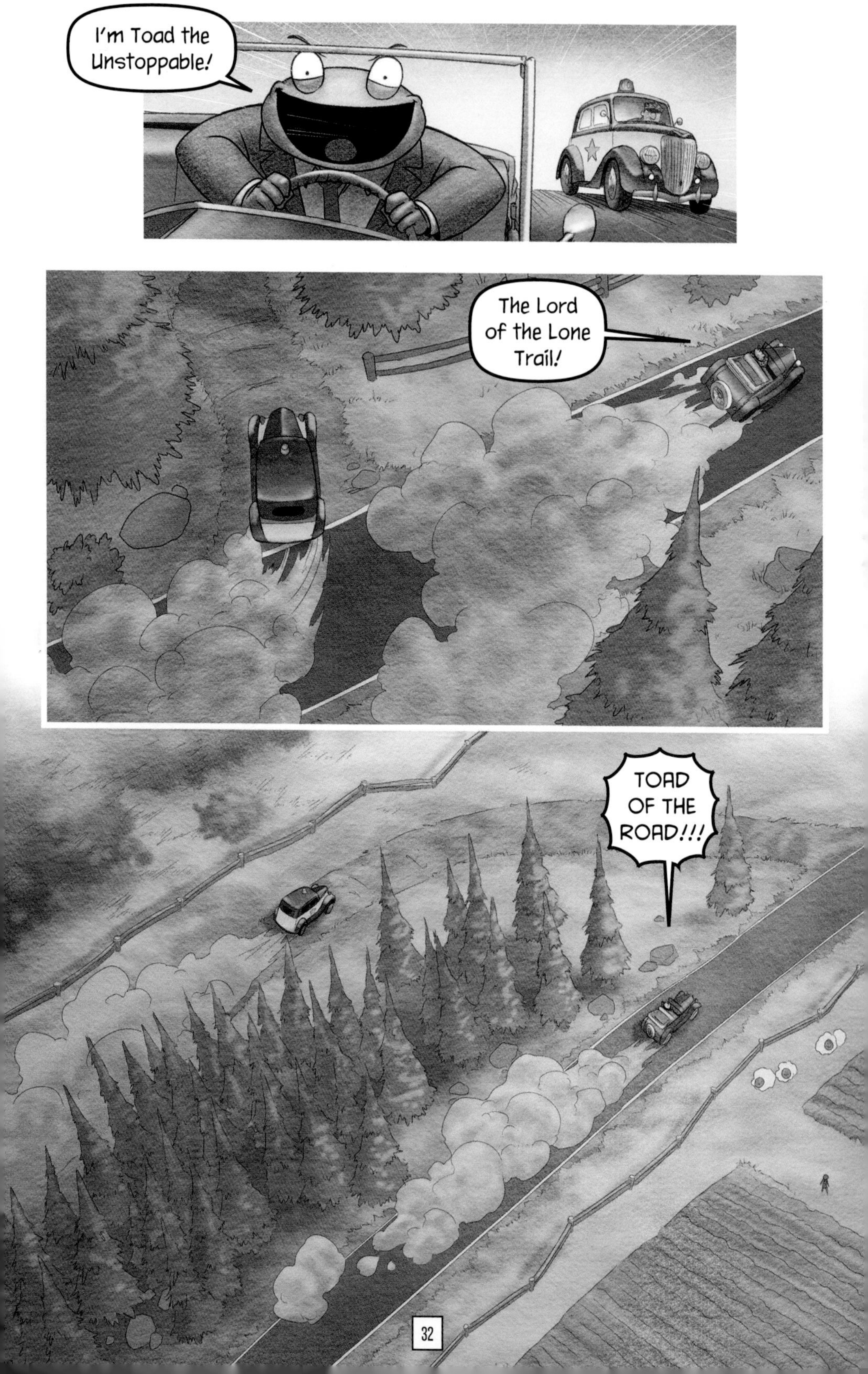
I'm Toad the Unstoppable!
The Lord of the Lone Trail!
TOAD OF THE ROAD!!!

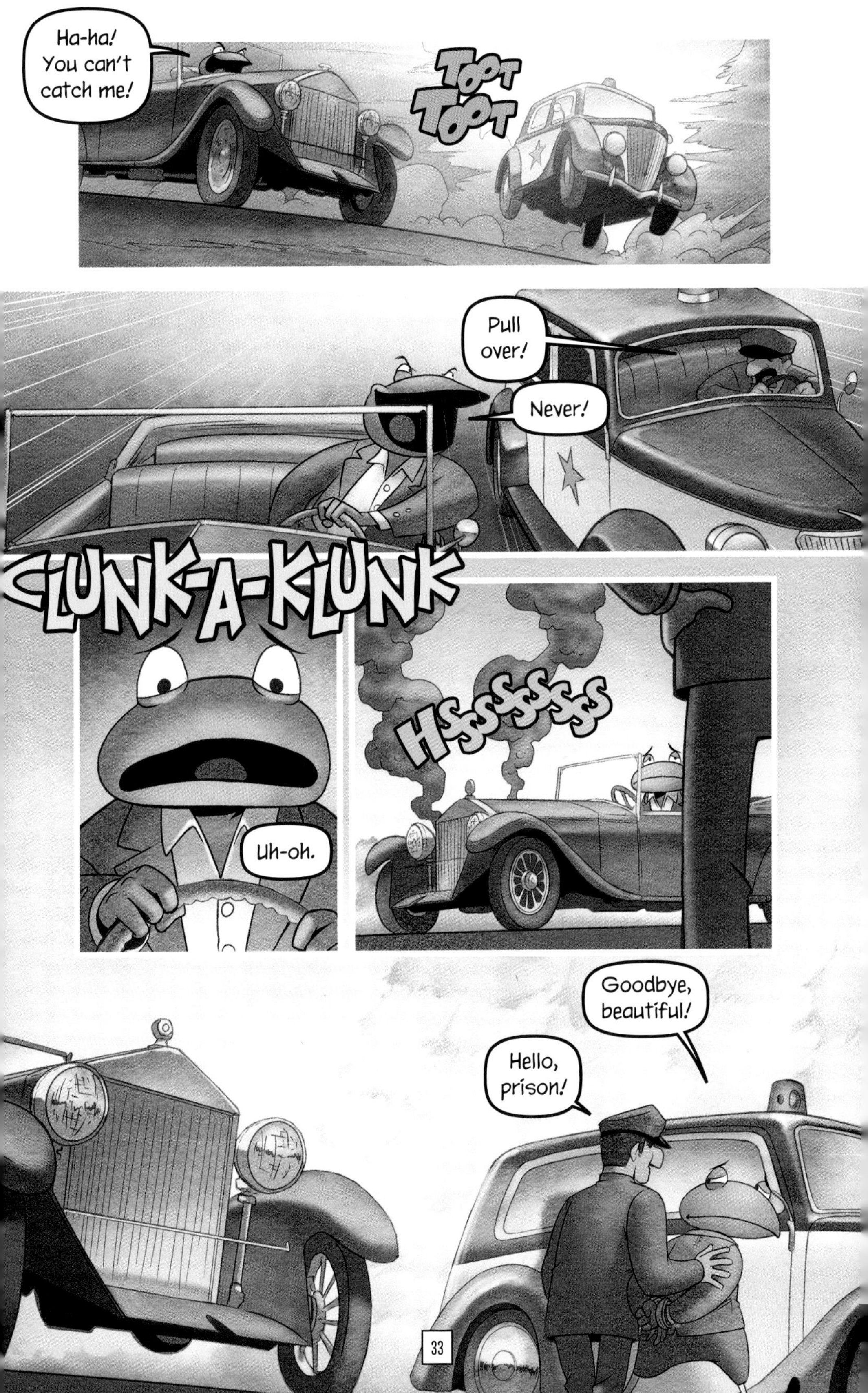
Ha-ha! You can't catch me!
TOOT TOOT
Pull over!
Never!
CLUNK-A-KLUNK
Uh-oh.
HSSSSSSS
Goodbye, beautiful!
Hello, prison!

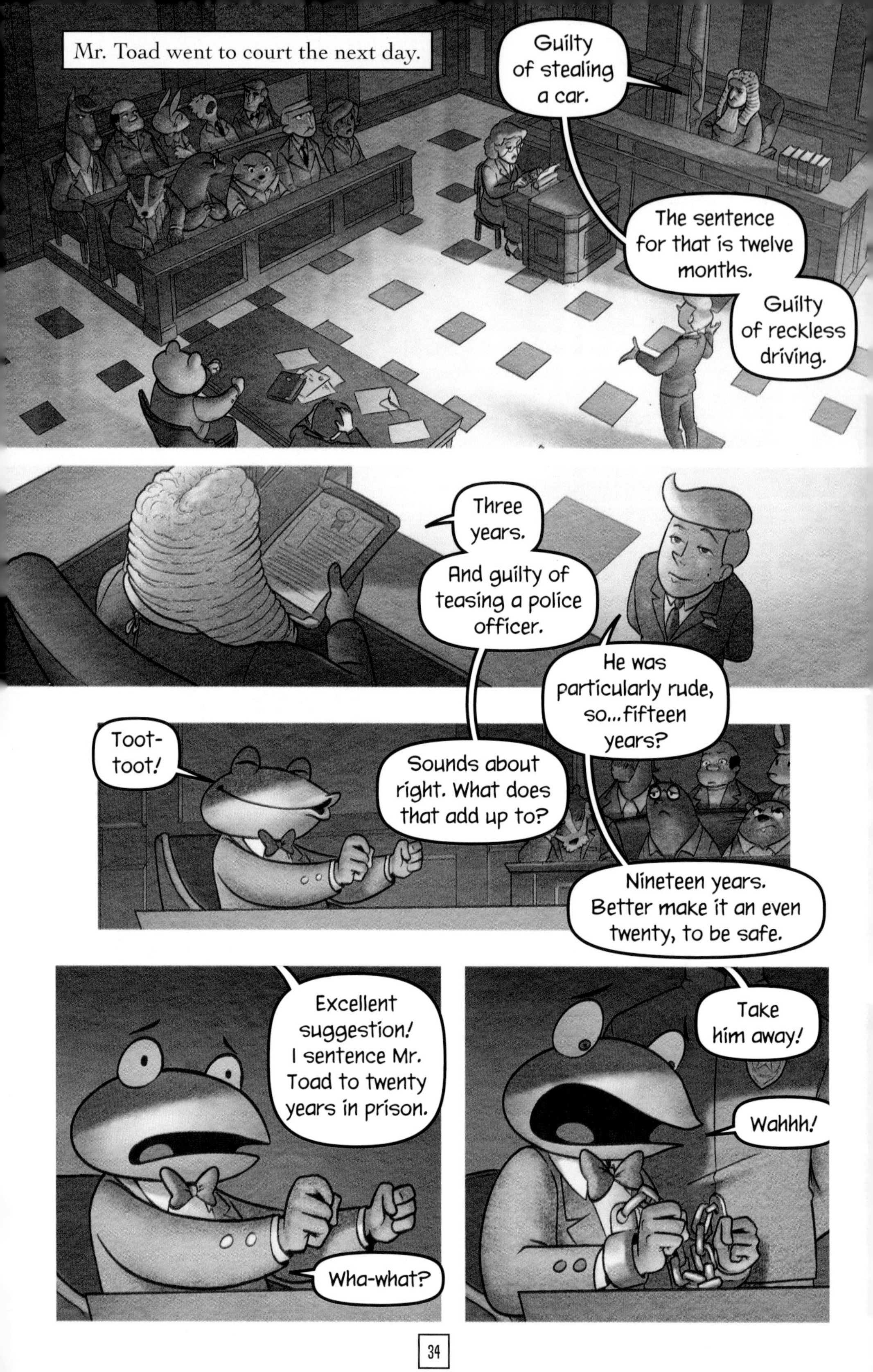
Mr. Toad went to court the next day.
Guilty of stealing a car.
The sentence for that is twelve months.
Guilty of reckless driving.
Three years.
And guilty of teasing a police officer.
He was particularly rude, so...fifteen years?
Toot-toot!
Sounds about right. What does that add up to?
Nineteen years. Better make it an even twenty, to be safe.
Excellent suggestion! I sentence Mr. Toad to twenty years in prison.
Wha-what?
Take him away!
Wahhh!

The officer led Mr. Toad out of the courthouse...

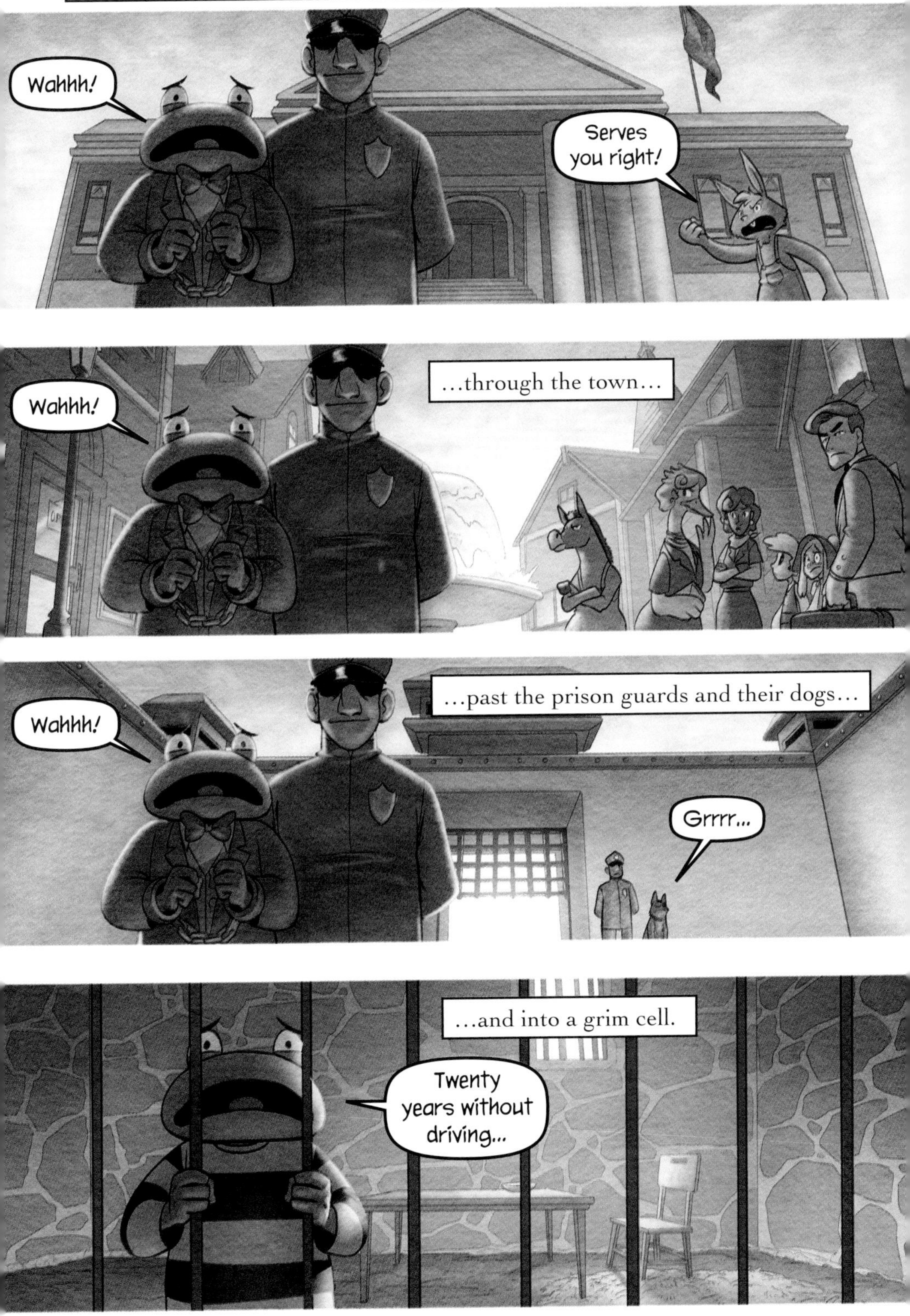
Wahhh!
Serves you right!
...through the town...
Wahhh!
...past the prison guards and their dogs...
Wahhh!
Grrrr...
...and into a grim cell.
Twenty years without driving...

CHAPTER 4
ESCAPE

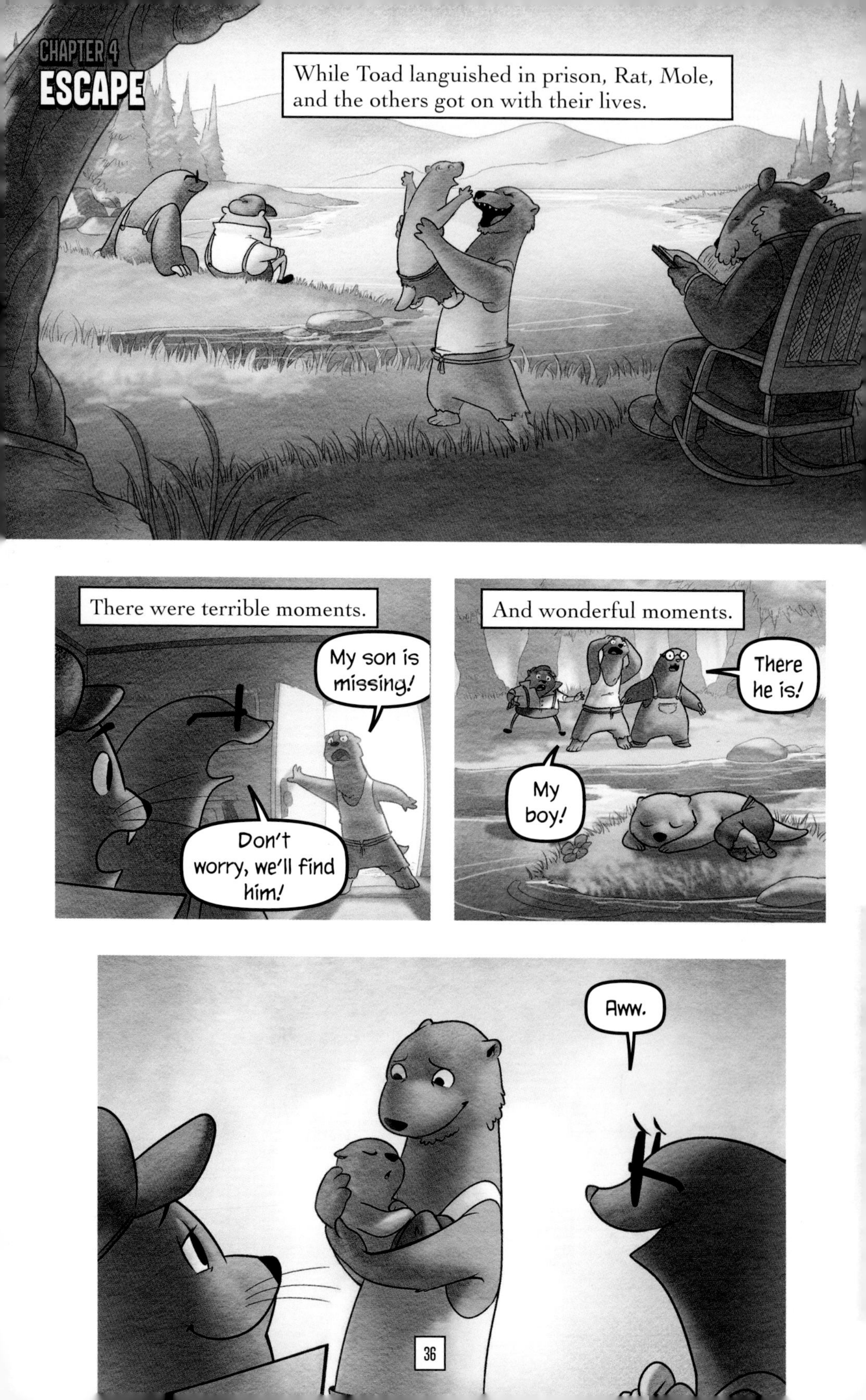
While Toad languished in prison, Rat, Mole, and the others got on with their lives.
There were terrible moments.
My son is missing!
Don't worry, we'll find him!
And wonderful moments.
There he is!
My boy!
Aww.

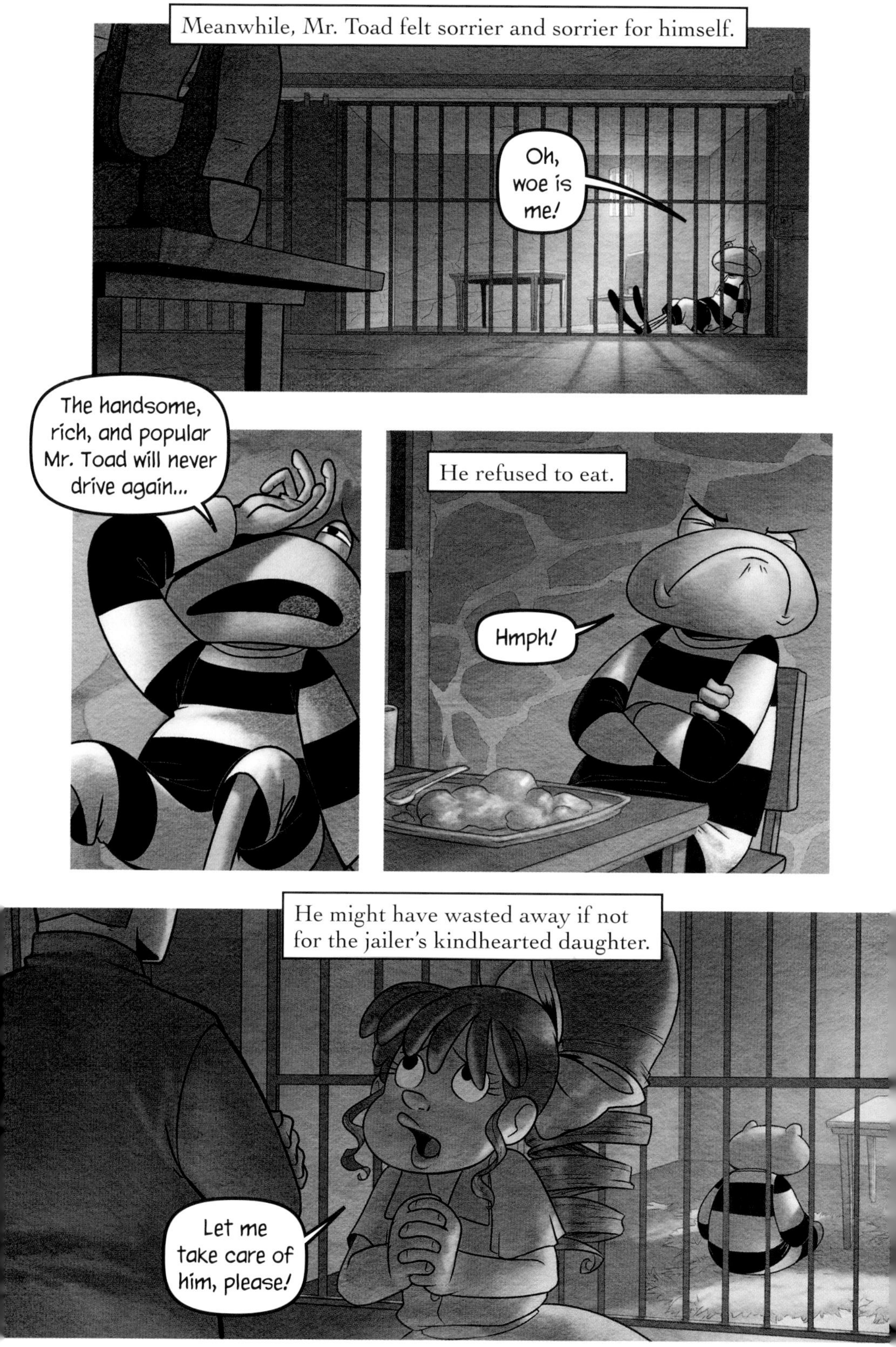
Meanwhile, Mr. Toad felt sorrier and sorrier for himself.
Oh, woe is me!
The handsome, rich, and popular Mr. Toad will never drive again...
He refused to eat.
Hmph!
He might have wasted away if not for the jailer's kindhearted daughter.
Let me take care of him, please!

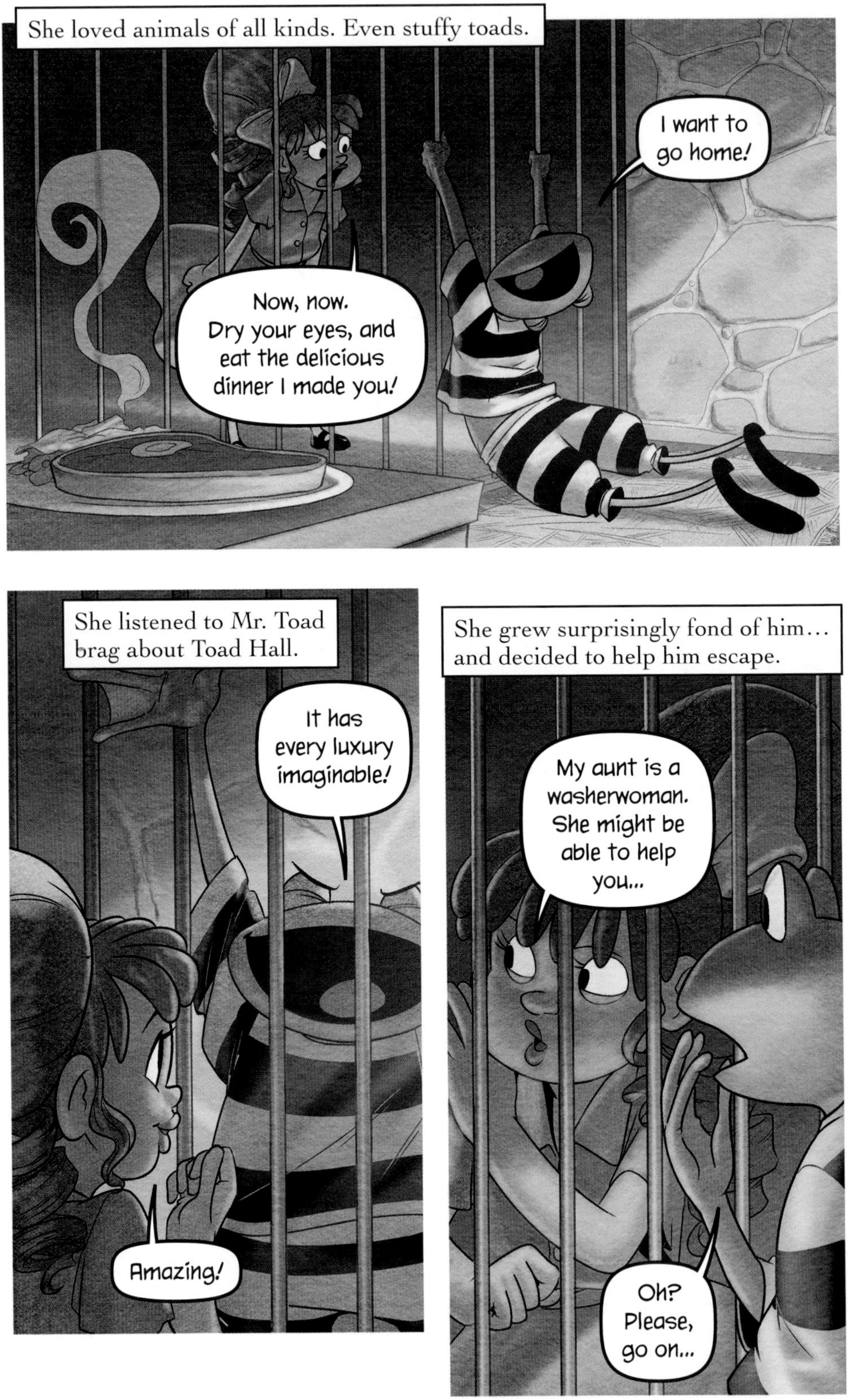
She loved animals of all kinds. Even stuffy toads.
I want to go home!
Now, now. Dry your eyes, and eat the delicious dinner I made you!
She listened to Mr. Toad brag about Toad Hall.
It has every luxury imaginable!
Amazing!
She grew surprisingly fond of him… and decided to help him escape.
My aunt is a washerwoman. She might be able to help you...
Oh? Please, go on...

The next evening, they put the plan in action.

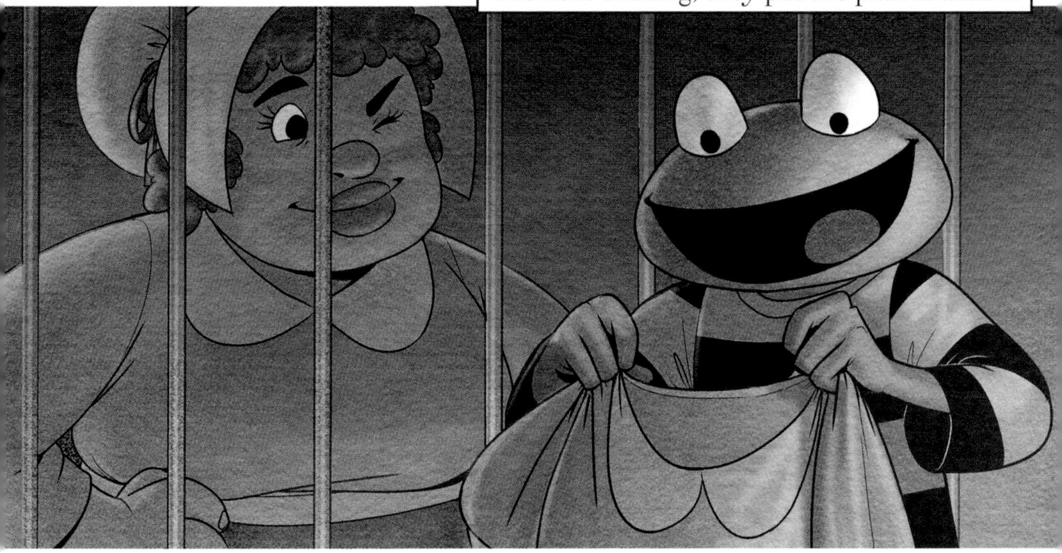

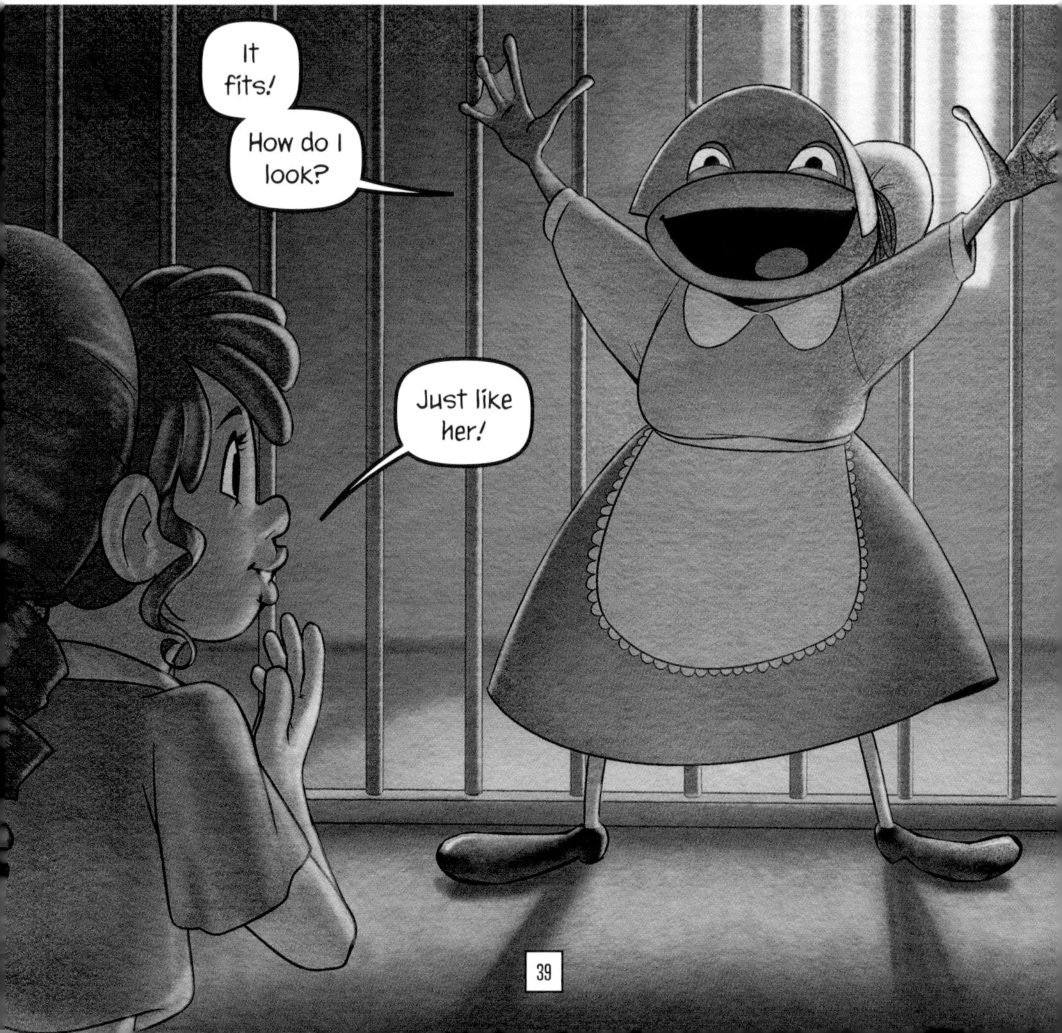
It fits!
How do I look?
Just like her!

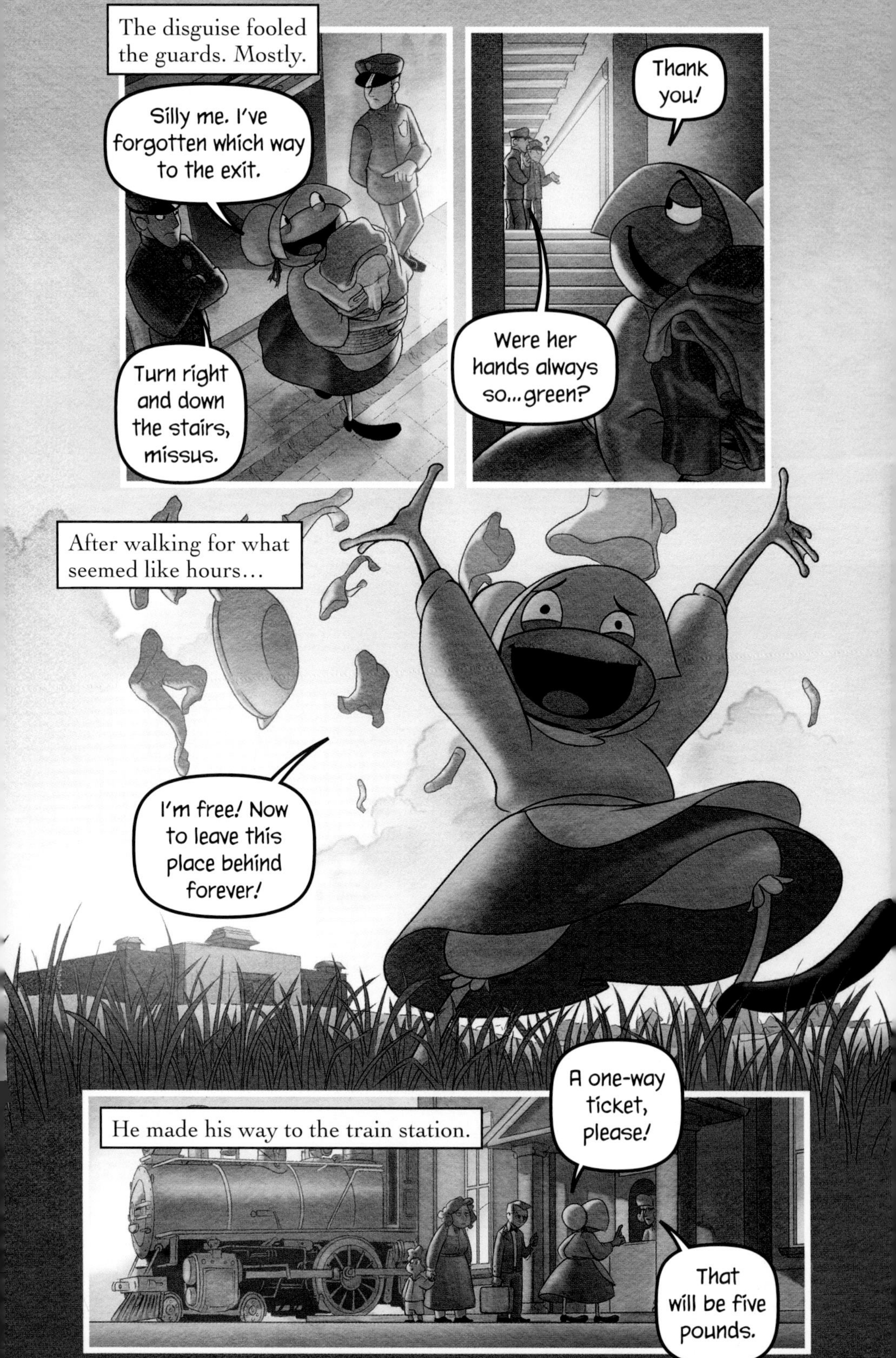

The disguise fooled the guards. Mostly.
Silly me. I've forgotten which way to the exit.
Turn right and down the stairs, missus.
Thank you!
Were her hands always so...green?
After walking for what seemed like hours...
I'm free! Now to leave this place behind forever!
He made his way to the train station.
A one-way ticket, please!
That will be five pounds.

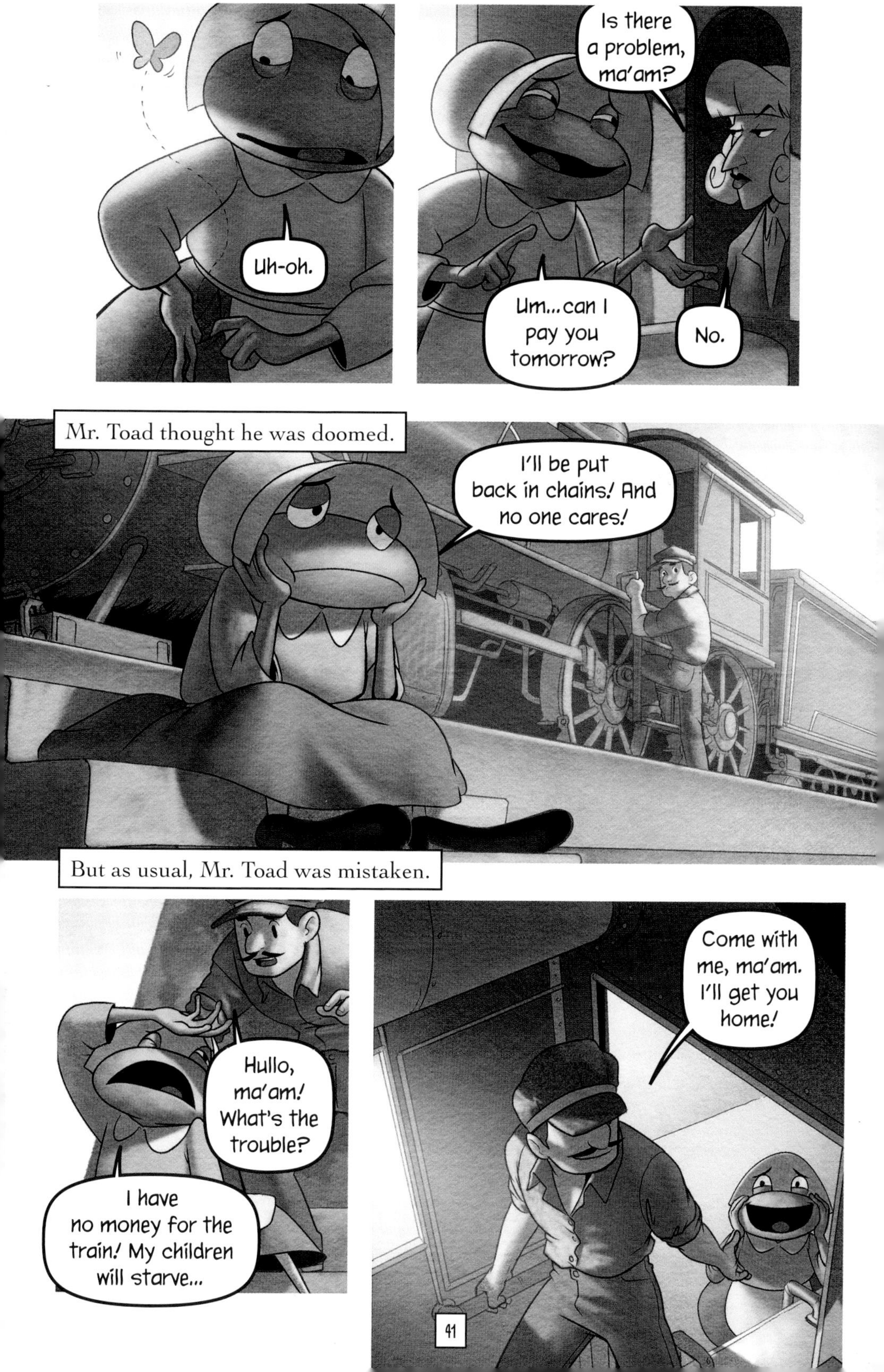
Uh-oh.
Is there a problem, ma'am?
Um...can I pay you tomorrow?
No.
Mr. Toad thought he was doomed.
I'll be put back in chains! And no one cares!
But as usual, Mr. Toad was mistaken.
Hullo, ma'am! What's the trouble?
I have no money for the train! My children will starve...
Come with me, ma'am. I'll get you home!

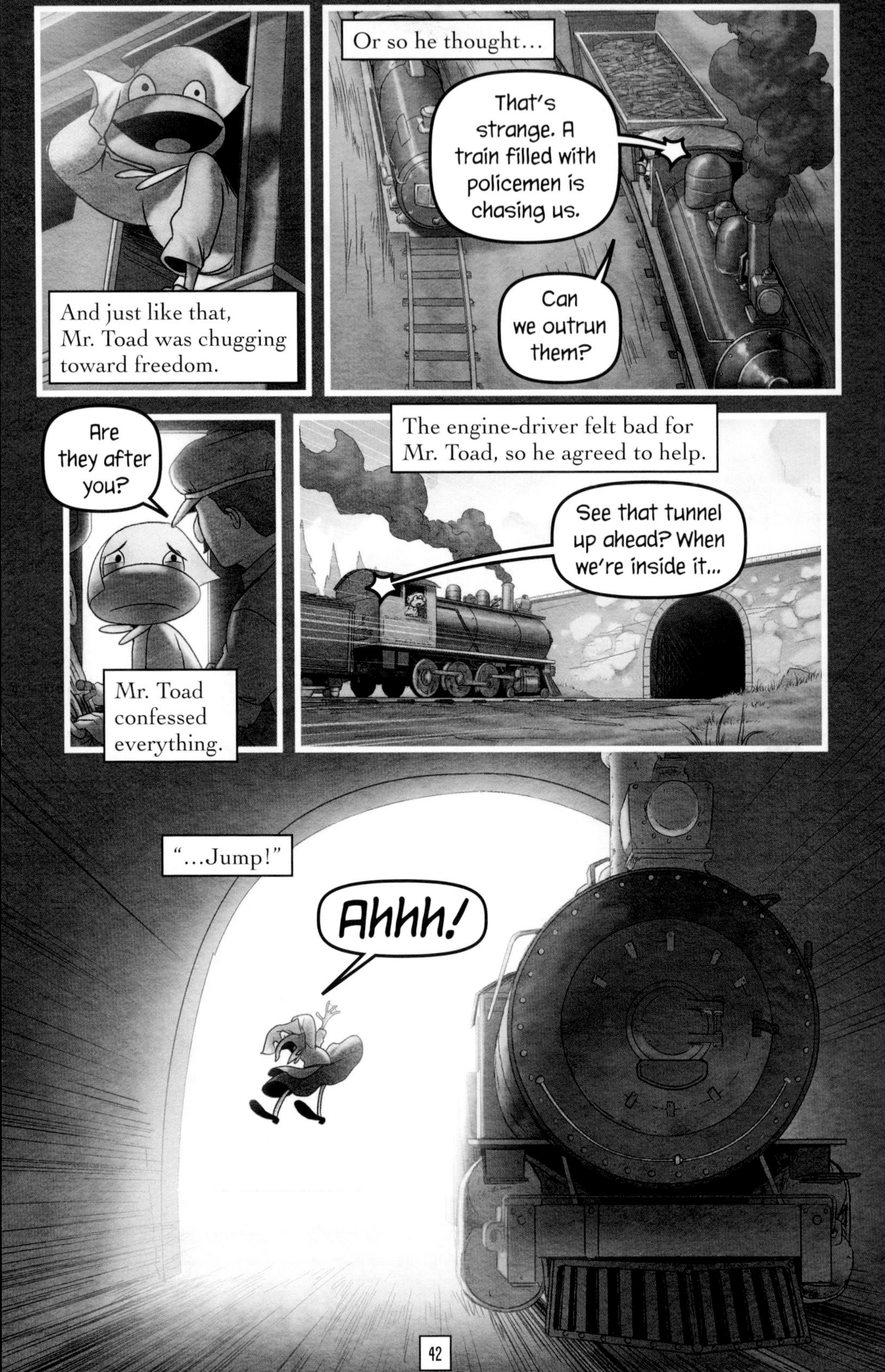

And just like that, Mr. Toad was chugging toward freedom.
Or so he thought…
That's strange. A train filled with policemen is chasing us.
Can we outrun them?
Are they after you?
Mr. Toad confessed everything.
The engine-driver felt bad for Mr. Toad, so he agreed to help.
See that tunnel up ahead? When we're inside it…
"…Jump!"
Ahhh!

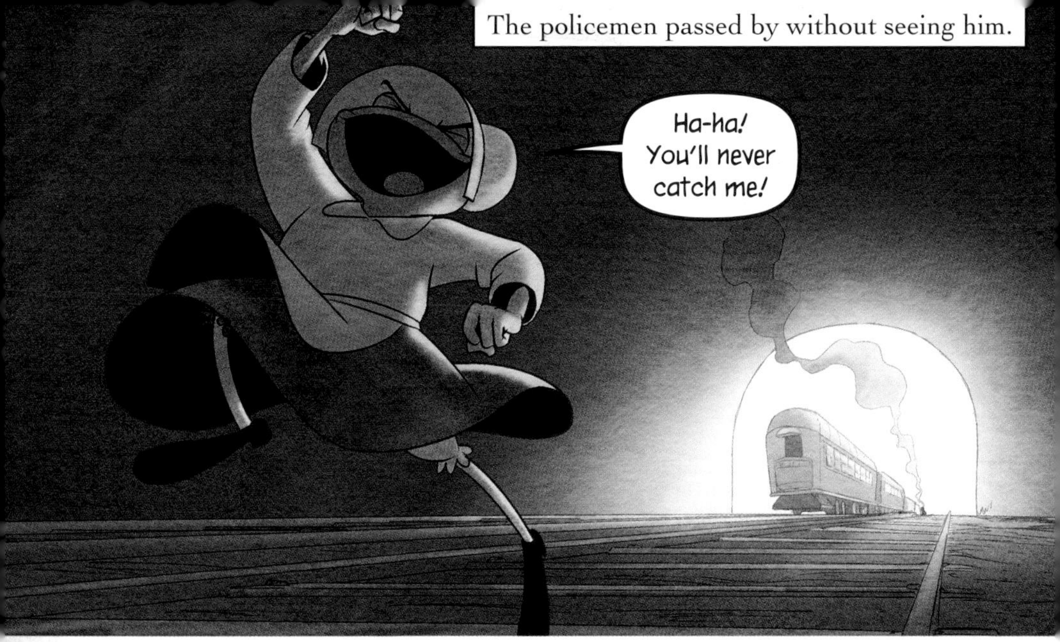
The policemen passed by without seeing him.
Ha-ha! You'll never catch me!

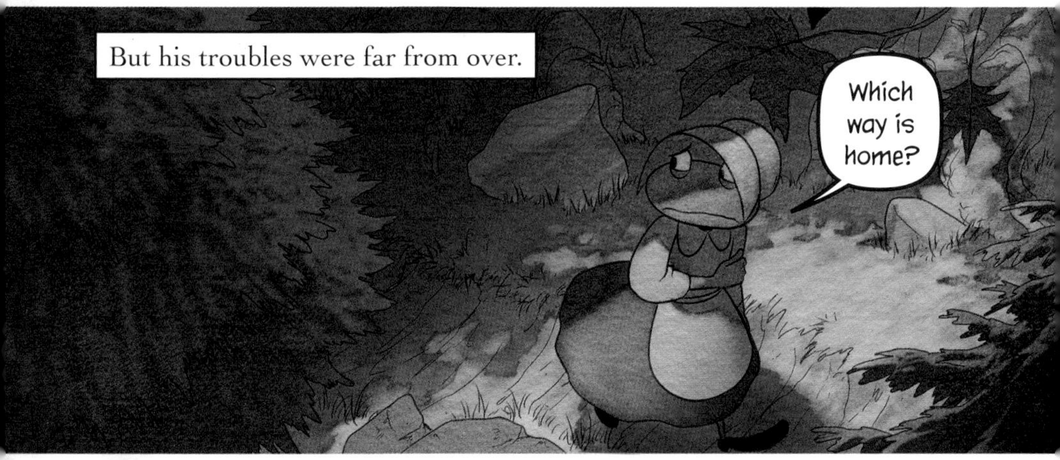
But his troubles were far from over.
Which way is home?

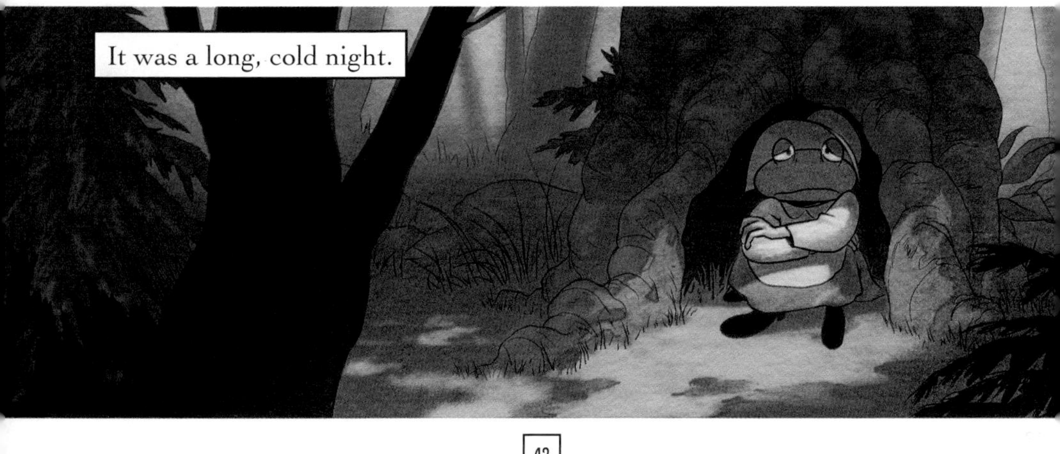
It was a long, cold night.

CHAPTER 5
ON THE RUN

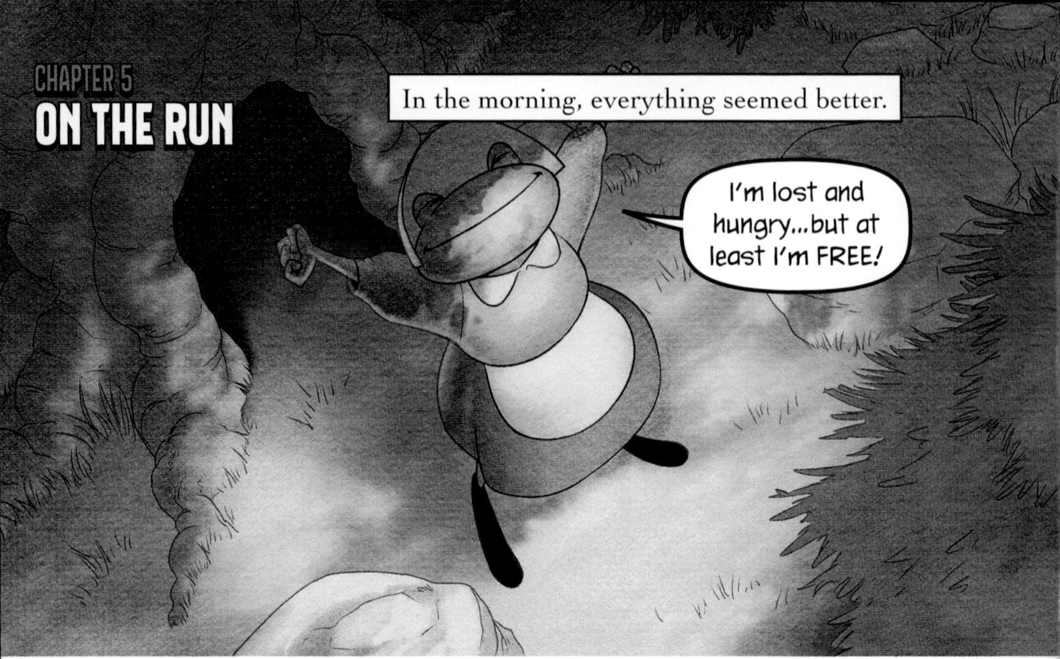
In the morning, everything seemed better.
I'm lost and hungry...but at least I'm FREE!

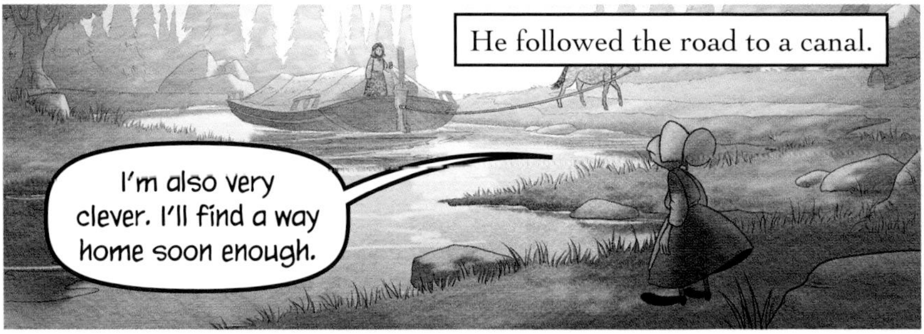
He followed the road to a canal.
I'm also very clever. I'll find a way home soon enough.

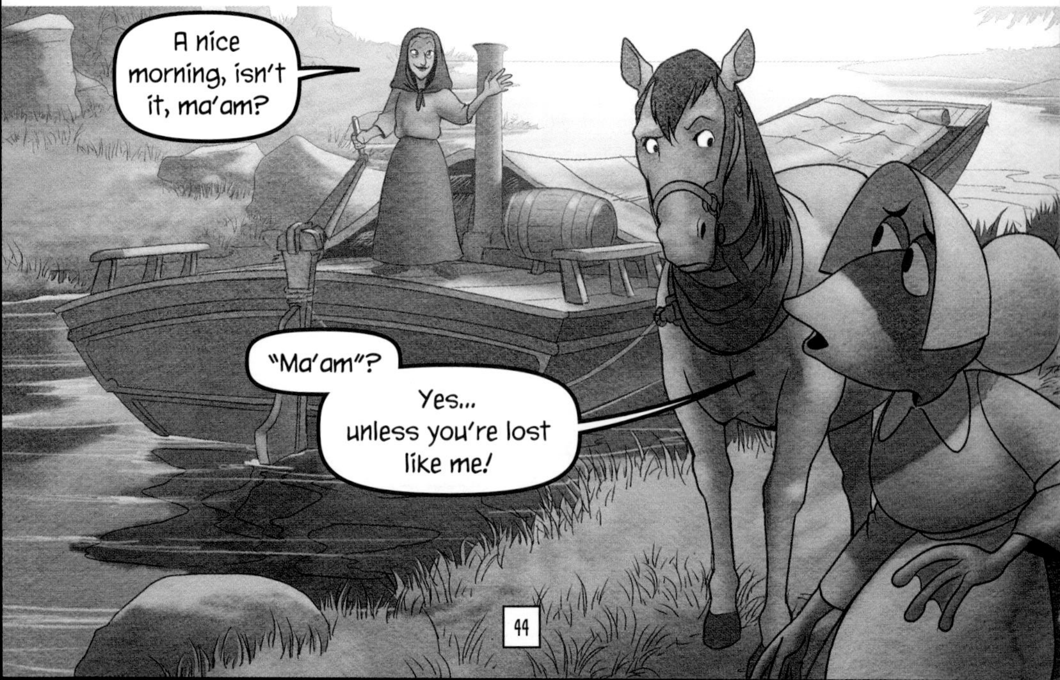
A nice morning, isn't it, ma'am?
"Ma'am"?
Yes... unless you're lost like me!

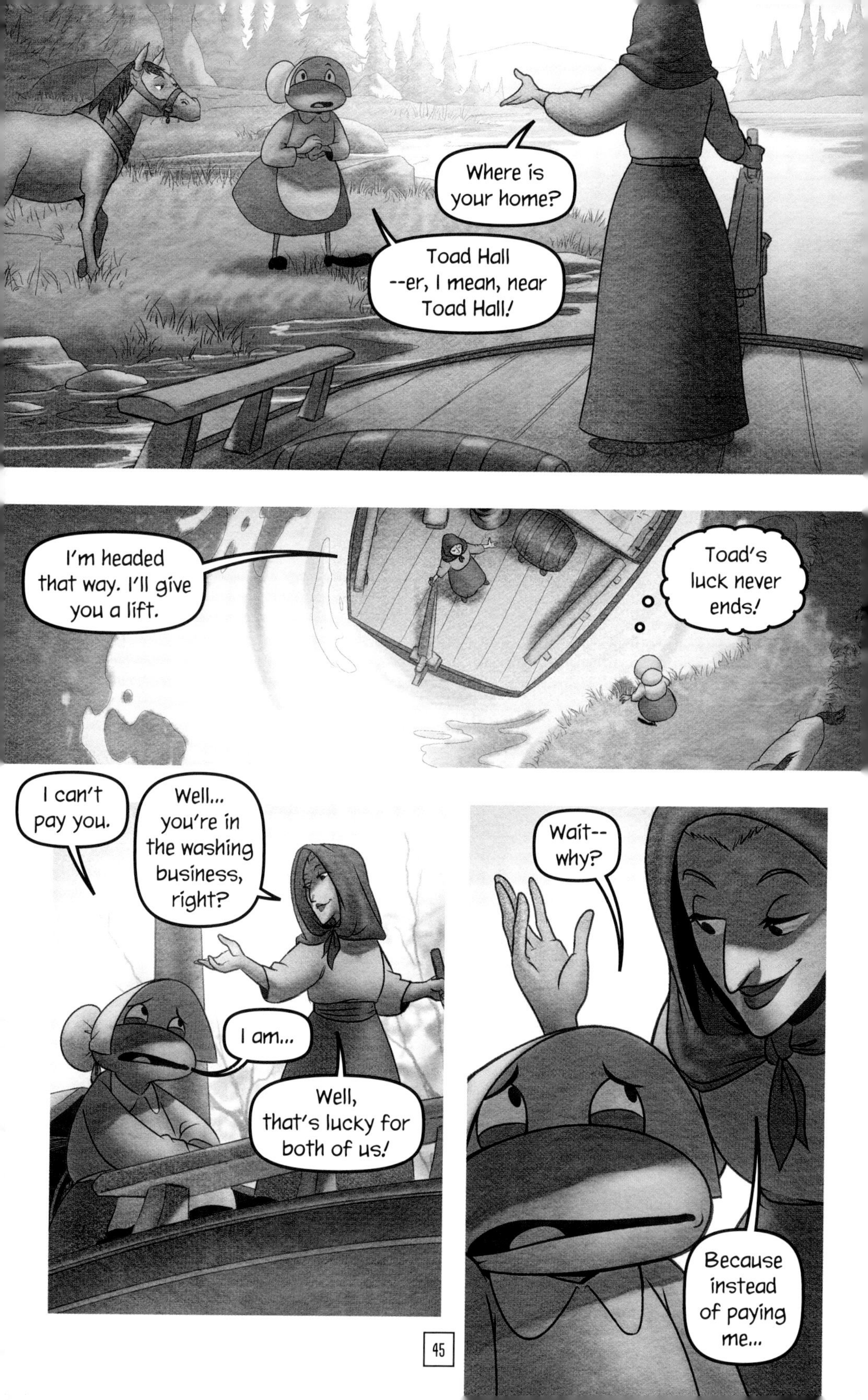
Where is your home?
Toad Hall --er, I mean, near Toad Hall!
I'm headed that way. I'll give you a lift.
Toad's luck never ends!
I can't pay you.
Well... you're in the washing business, right?
I am...
Well, that's lucky for both of us!
Wait--why?
Because instead of paying me...

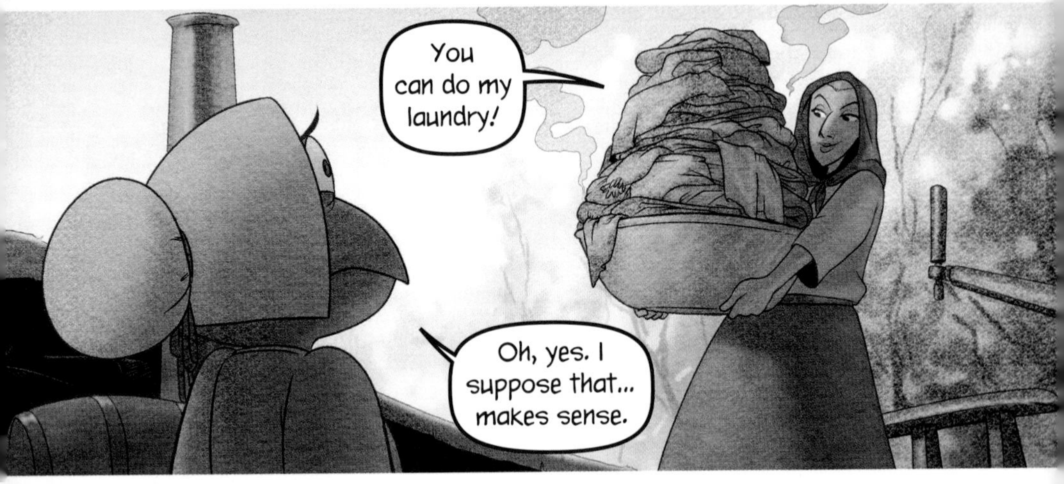
You can do my laundry!
Oh, yes. I suppose that... makes sense.

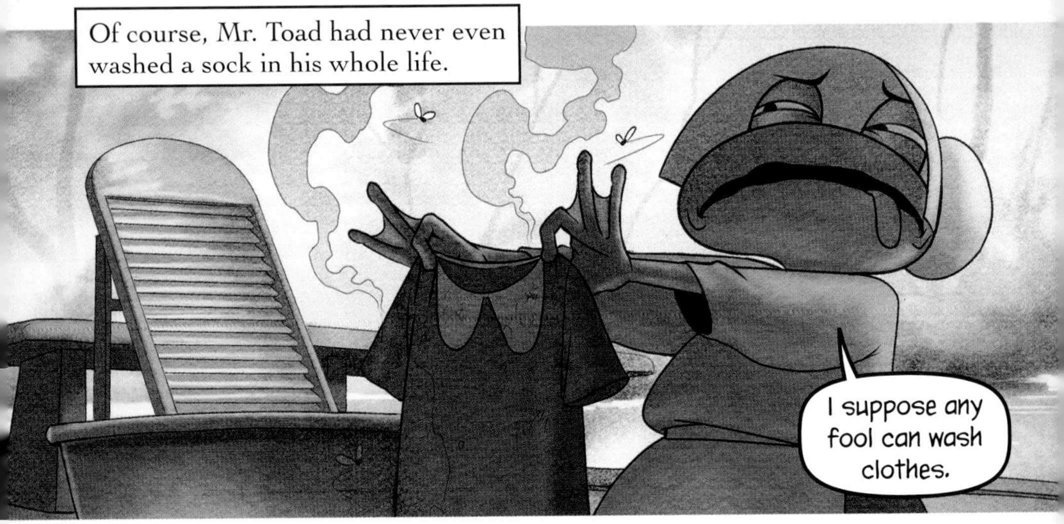
Of course, Mr. Toad had never even washed a sock in his whole life.
I suppose any fool can wash clothes.

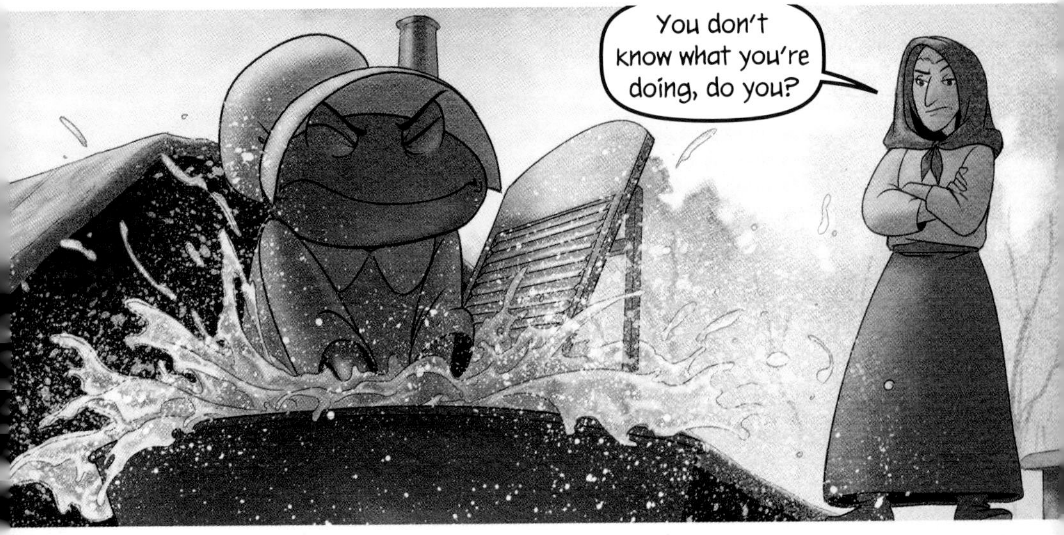
You don't know what you're doing, do you?

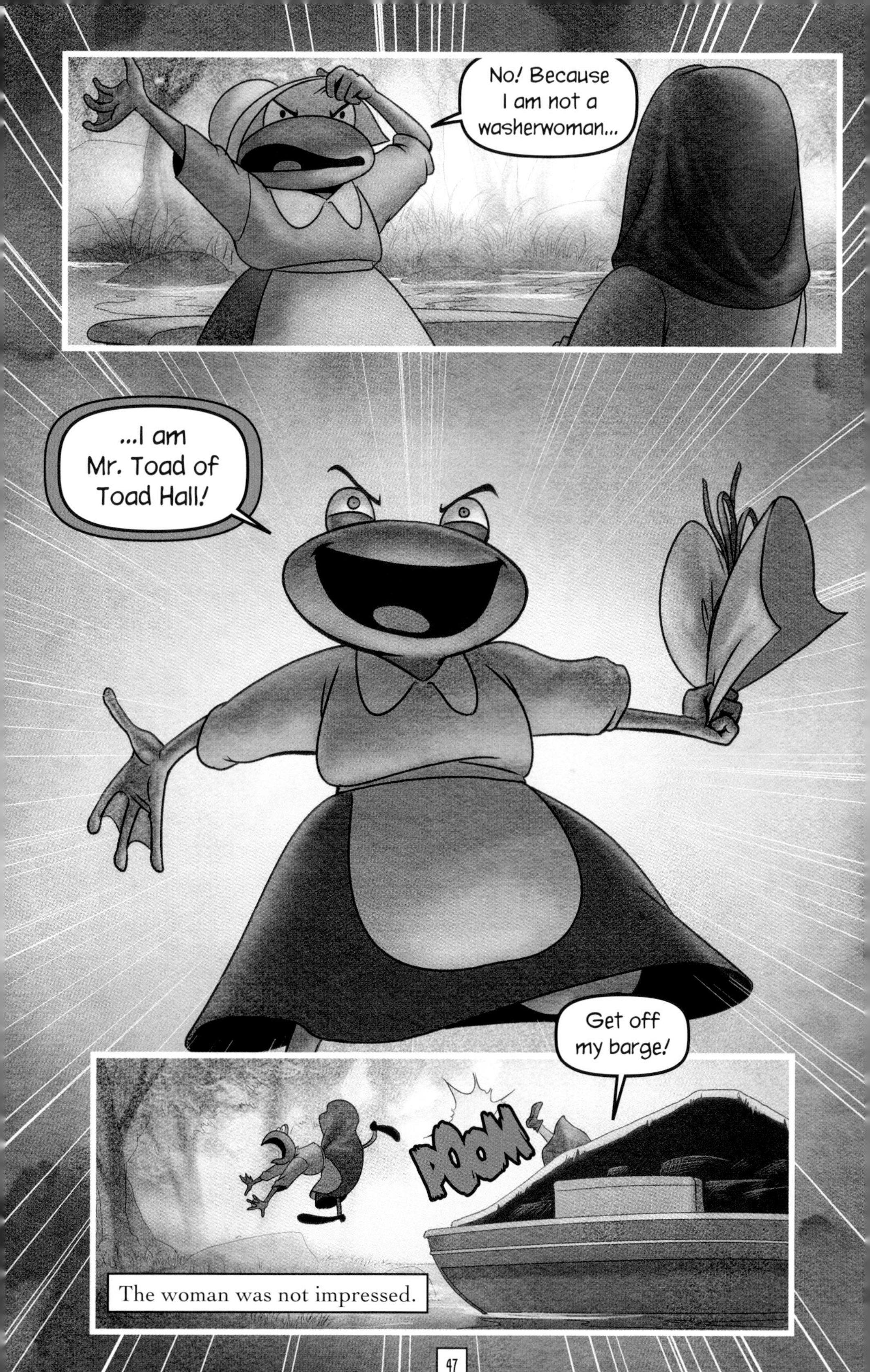
No! Because I am not a washerwoman...
...I am Mr. Toad of Toad Hall!
Get off my barge!
POOM
The woman was not impressed.

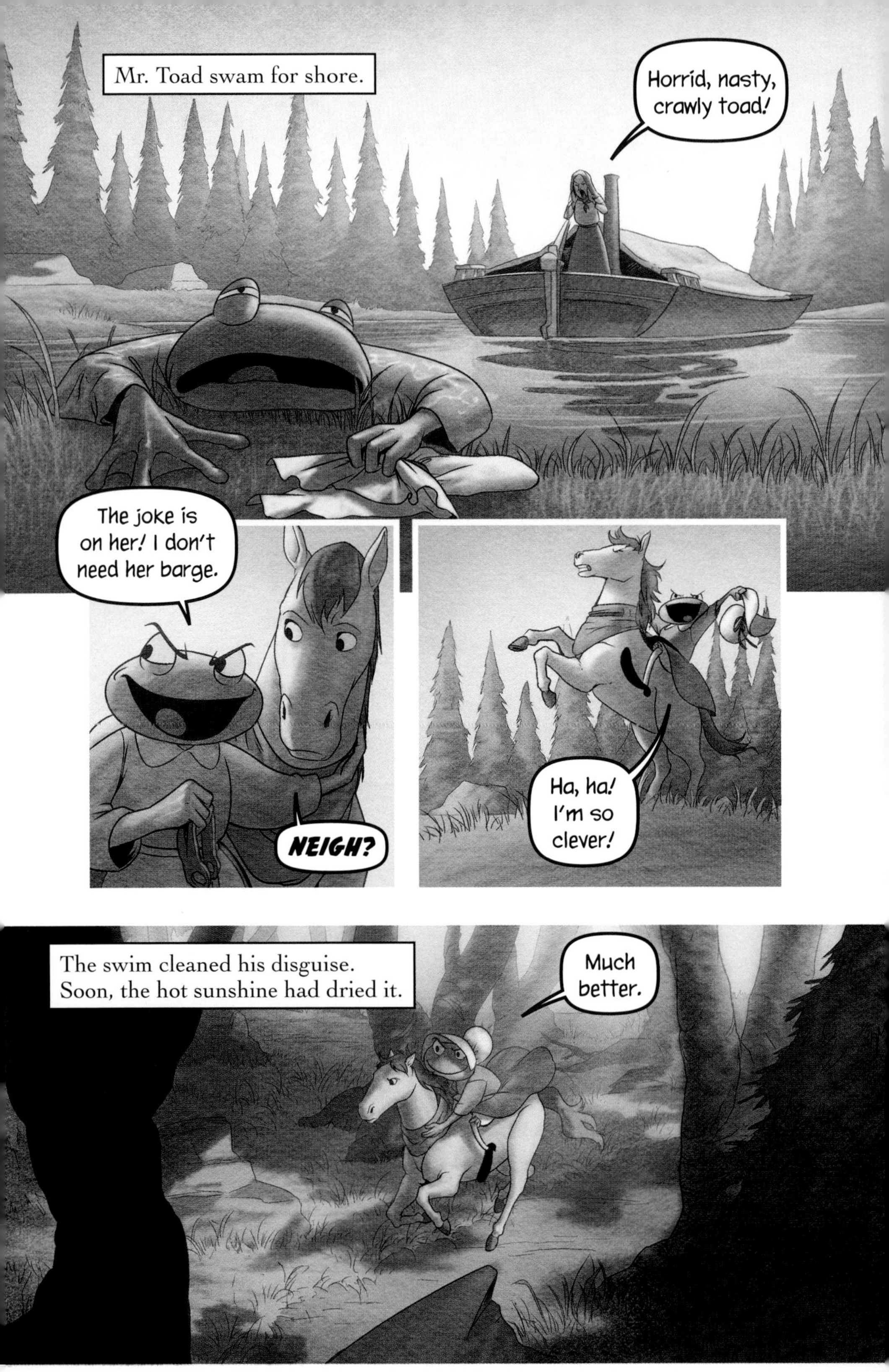
Mr. Toad swam for shore.
Horrid, nasty, crawly toad!
The joke is on her! I don't need her barge.
NEIGH?
Ha, ha! I'm so clever!
The swim cleaned his disguise. Soon, the hot sunshine had dried it.
Much better.

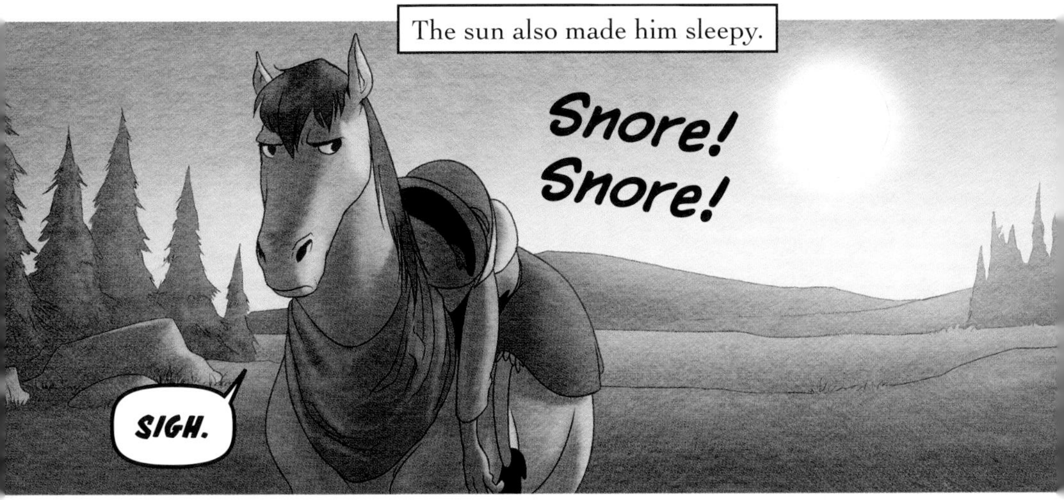
The sun also made him sleepy.
Snore! Snore!
SIGH.

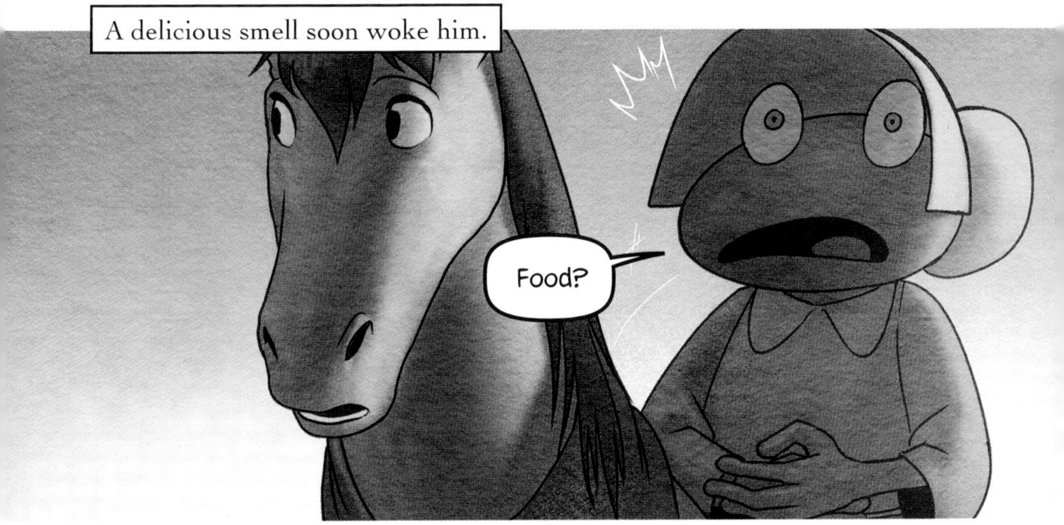
A delicious smell soon woke him.
Food?

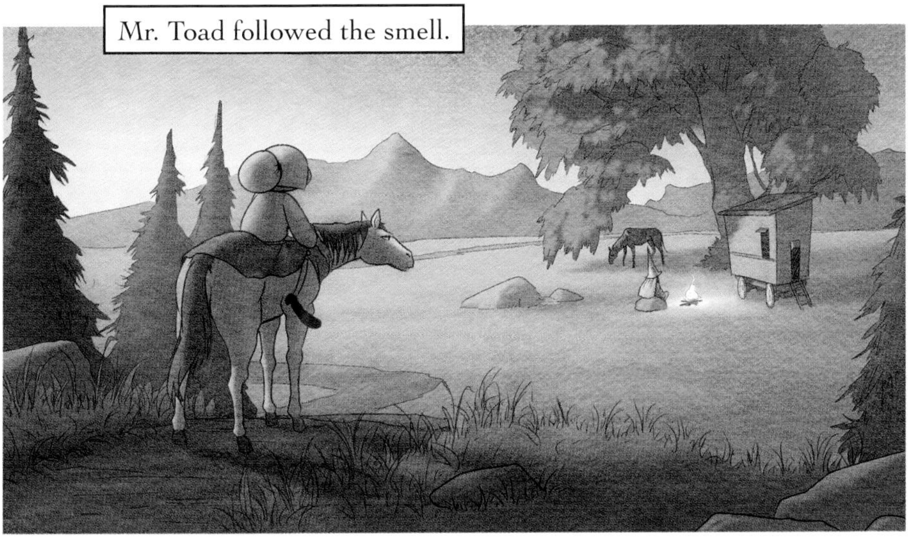
Mr. Toad followed the smell.

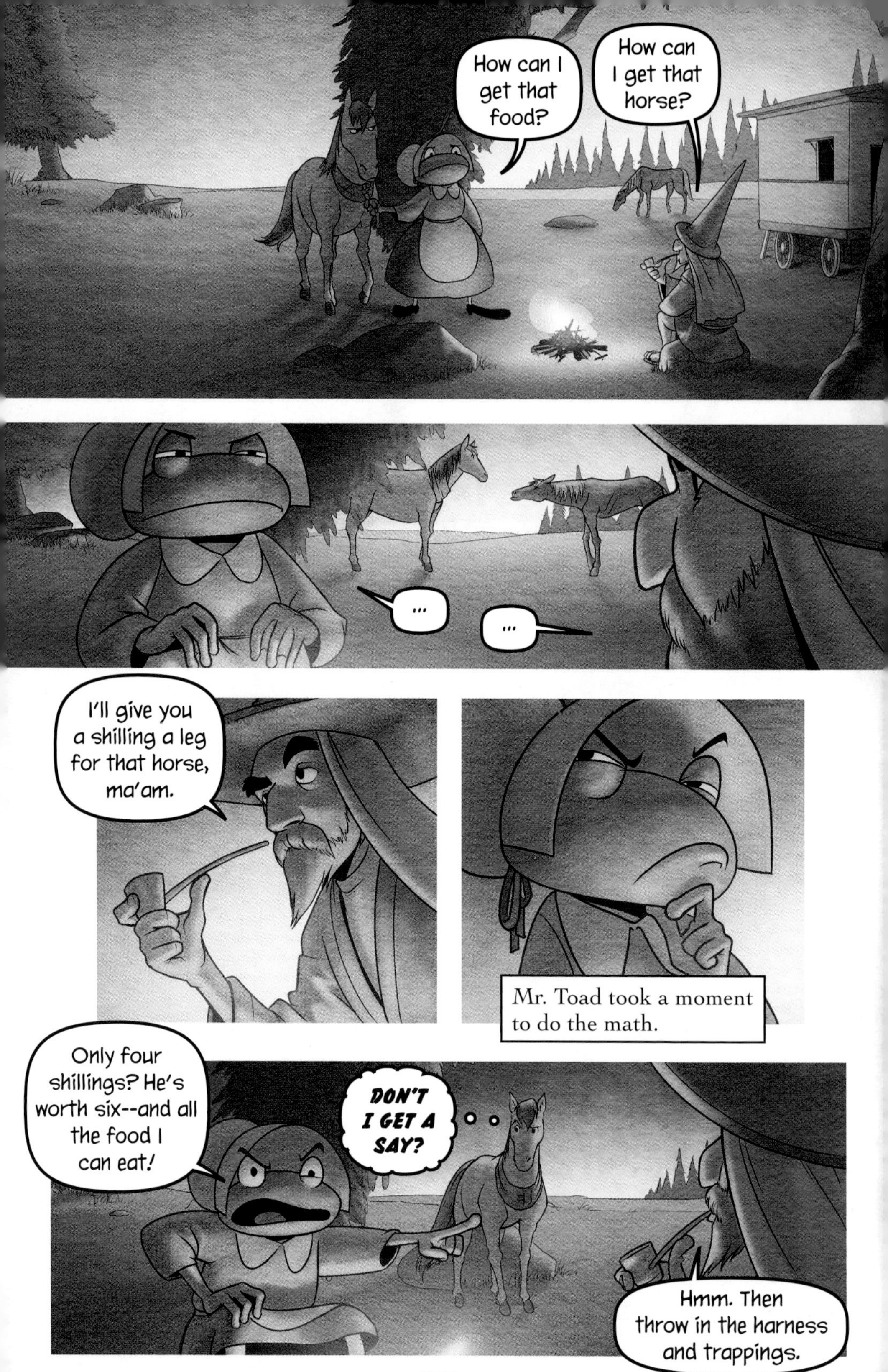
How can I get that food?
How can I get that horse?
...
...
I'll give you a shilling a leg for that horse, ma'am.
Mr. Toad took a moment to do the math.
Only four shillings? He's worth six--and all the food I can eat!
DON'T I GET A SAY?
Hmm. Then throw in the harness and trappings.

Mr. Toad pocketed the coins.

He helped himself to the stew.

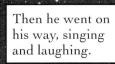

Then he went on his way, singing and laughing.

Oh, I am so clever!

Oh, nothing can stop me!

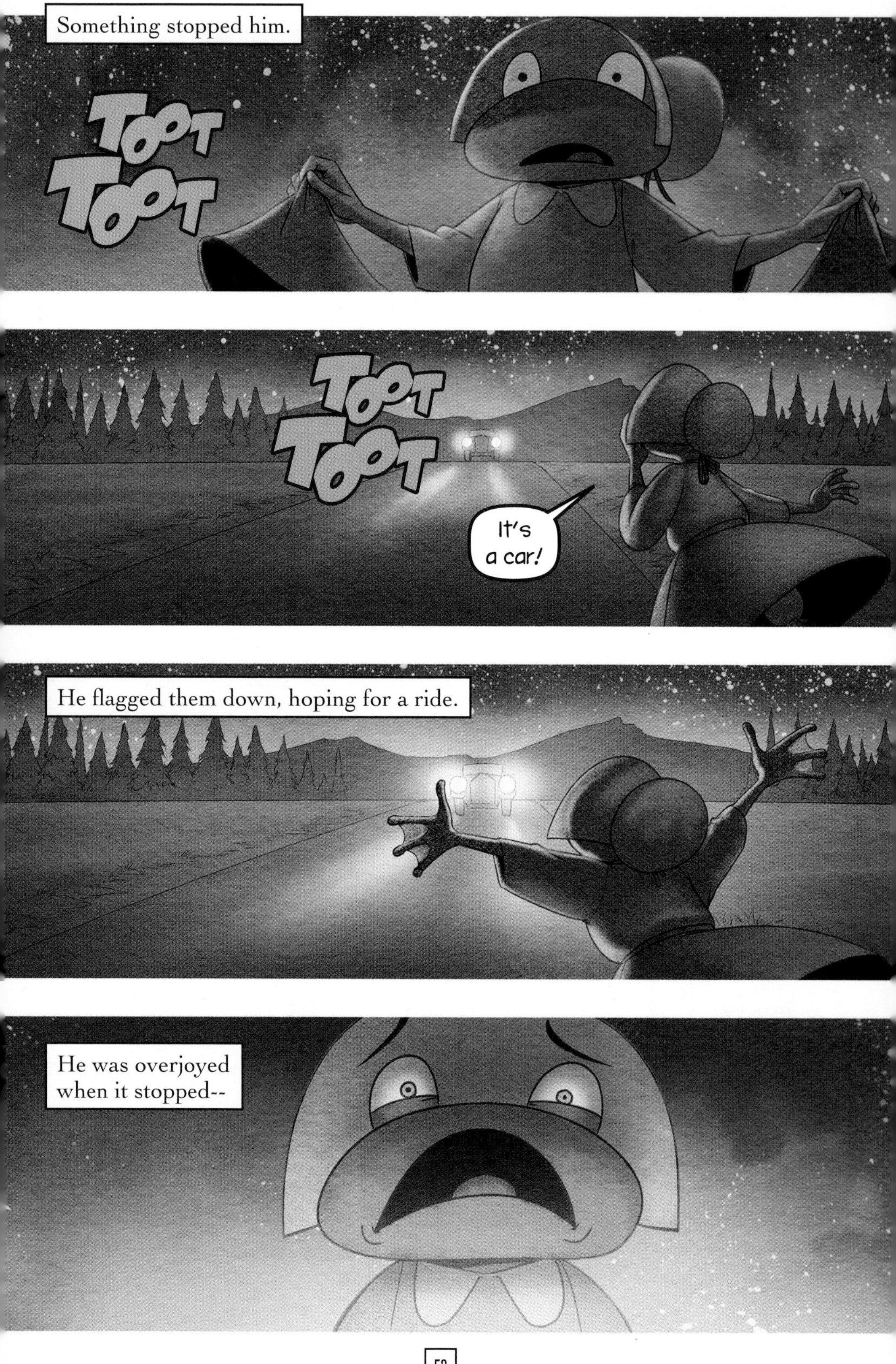
Something stopped him.
TOOT TOOT
TOOT TOOT
It's a car!
He flagged them down, hoping for a ride.
He was overjoyed when it stopped--

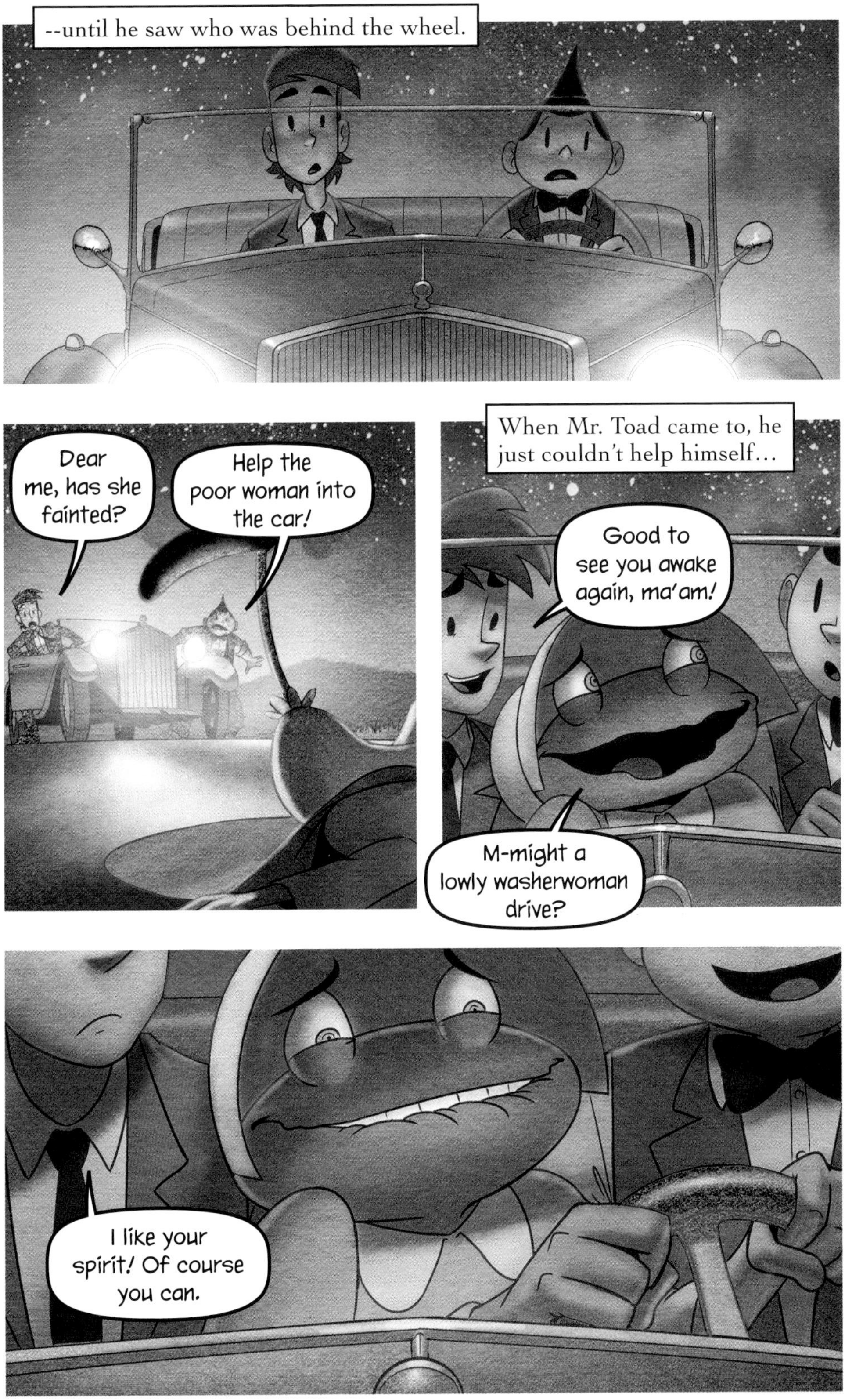
--until he saw who was behind the wheel.
Dear me, has she fainted?
Help the poor woman into the car!
When Mr. Toad came to, he just couldn't help himself...
Good to see you awake again, ma'am!
M-might a lowly washerwoman drive?
I like your spirit! Of course you can.

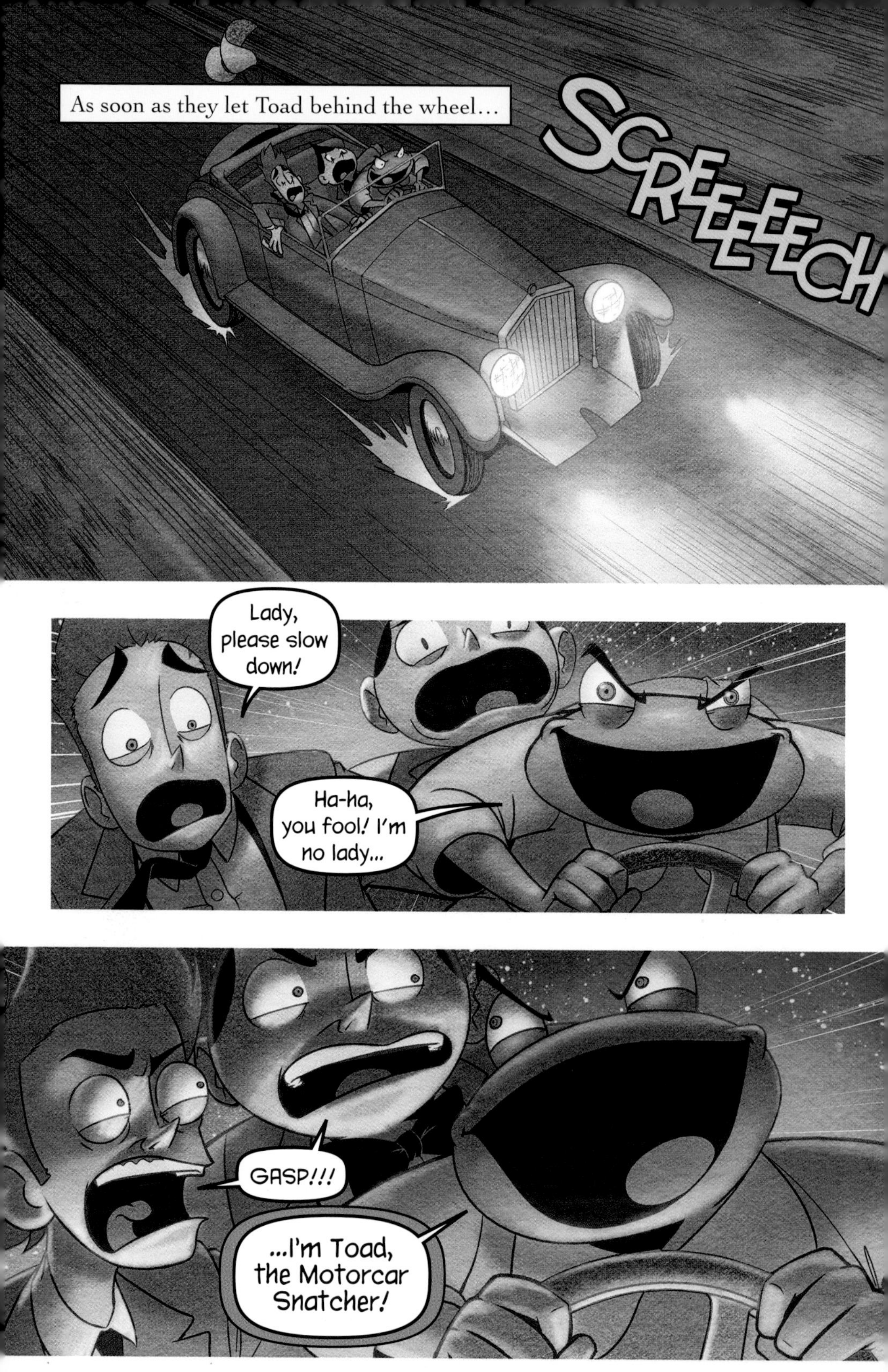

As soon as they let Toad behind the wheel...
SCREEEEECH
Lady, please slow down!
Ha-ha, you fool! I'm no lady...
GASP!!!
...I'm Toad, the Motorcar Snatcher!

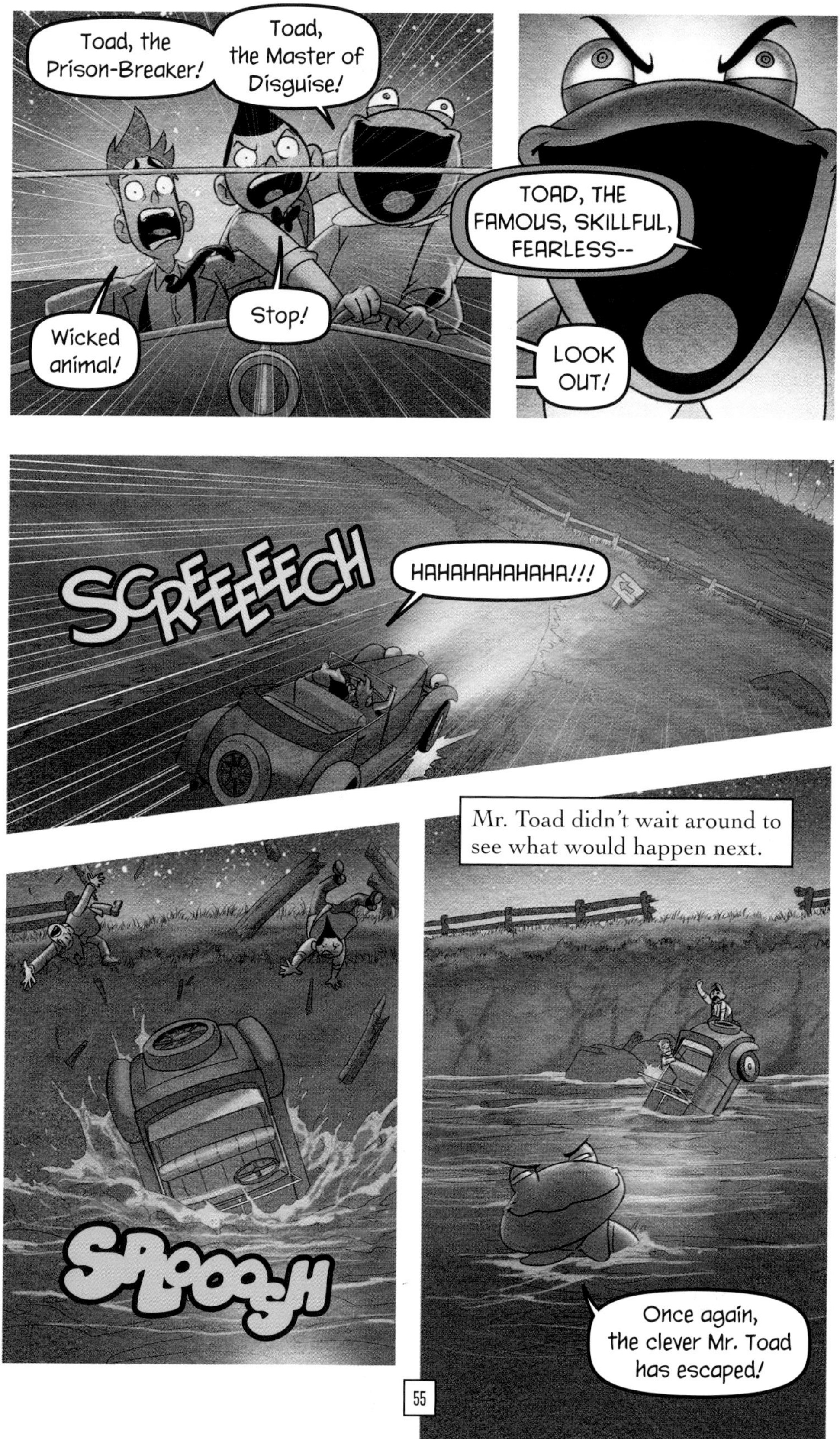

Toad, the Prison-Breaker!
Toad, the Master of Disguise!
Wicked animal!
Stop!
TOAD, THE FAMOUS, SKILLFUL, FEARLESS--
LOOK OUT!
SCREEEEECH
HAHAHAHAHAHA!!!
SPLOOOSH
Mr. Toad didn't wait around to see what would happen next.
Once again, the clever Mr. Toad has escaped!

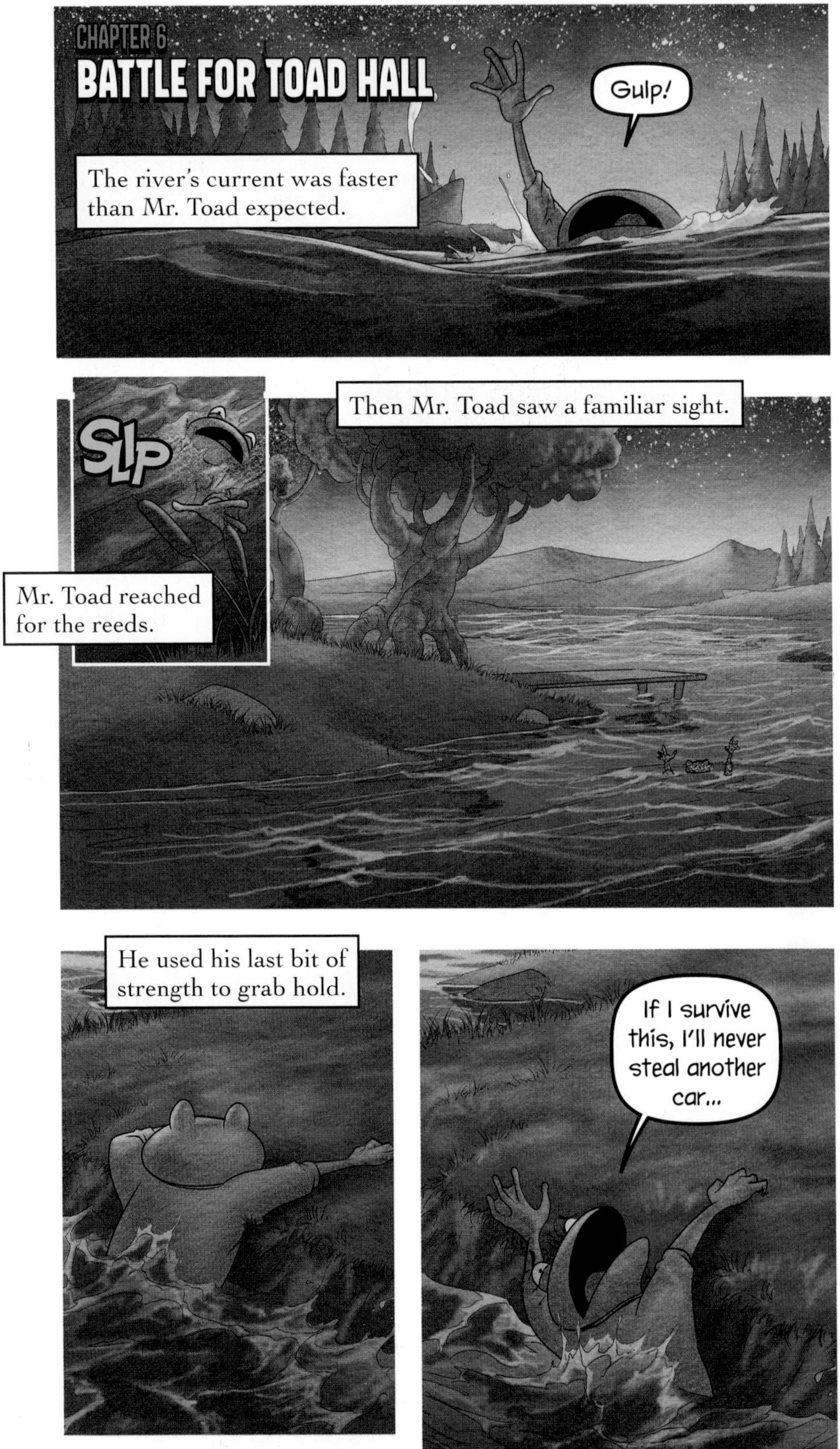
CHAPTER 6
BATTLE FOR TOAD HALL
The river's current was faster than Mr. Toad expected.
Gulp!
SLIP
Mr. Toad reached for the reeds.
Then Mr. Toad saw a familiar sight.
He used his last bit of strength to grab hold.
If I survive this, I'll never steal another car...

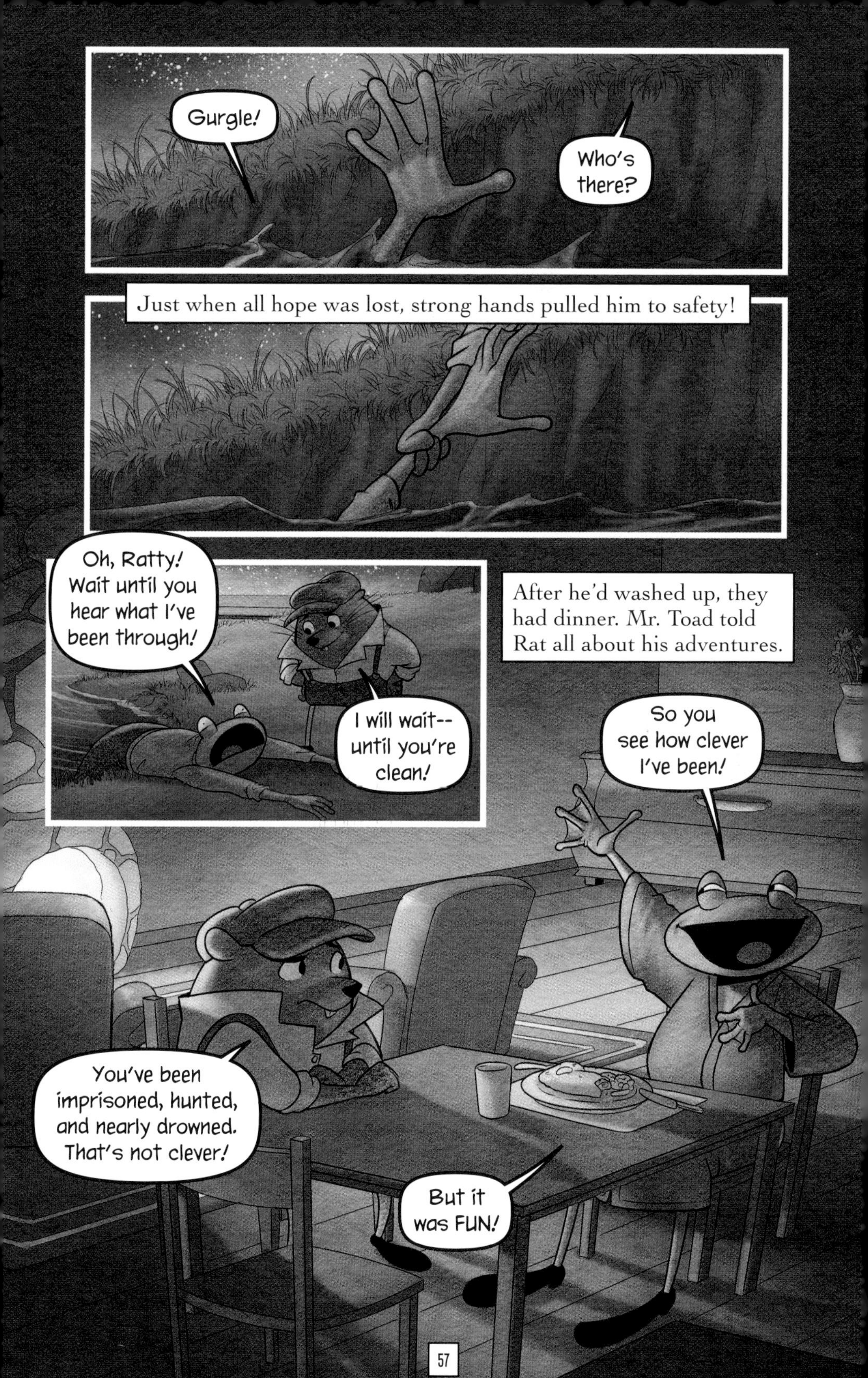
Gurgle!
Who's there?
Just when all hope was lost, strong hands pulled him to safety!
Oh, Ratty! Wait until you hear what I've been through!
I will wait-- until you're clean!
After he'd washed up, they had dinner. Mr. Toad told Rat all about his adventures.
So you see how clever I've been!
You've been imprisoned, hunted, and nearly drowned. That's not clever!
But it was FUN!

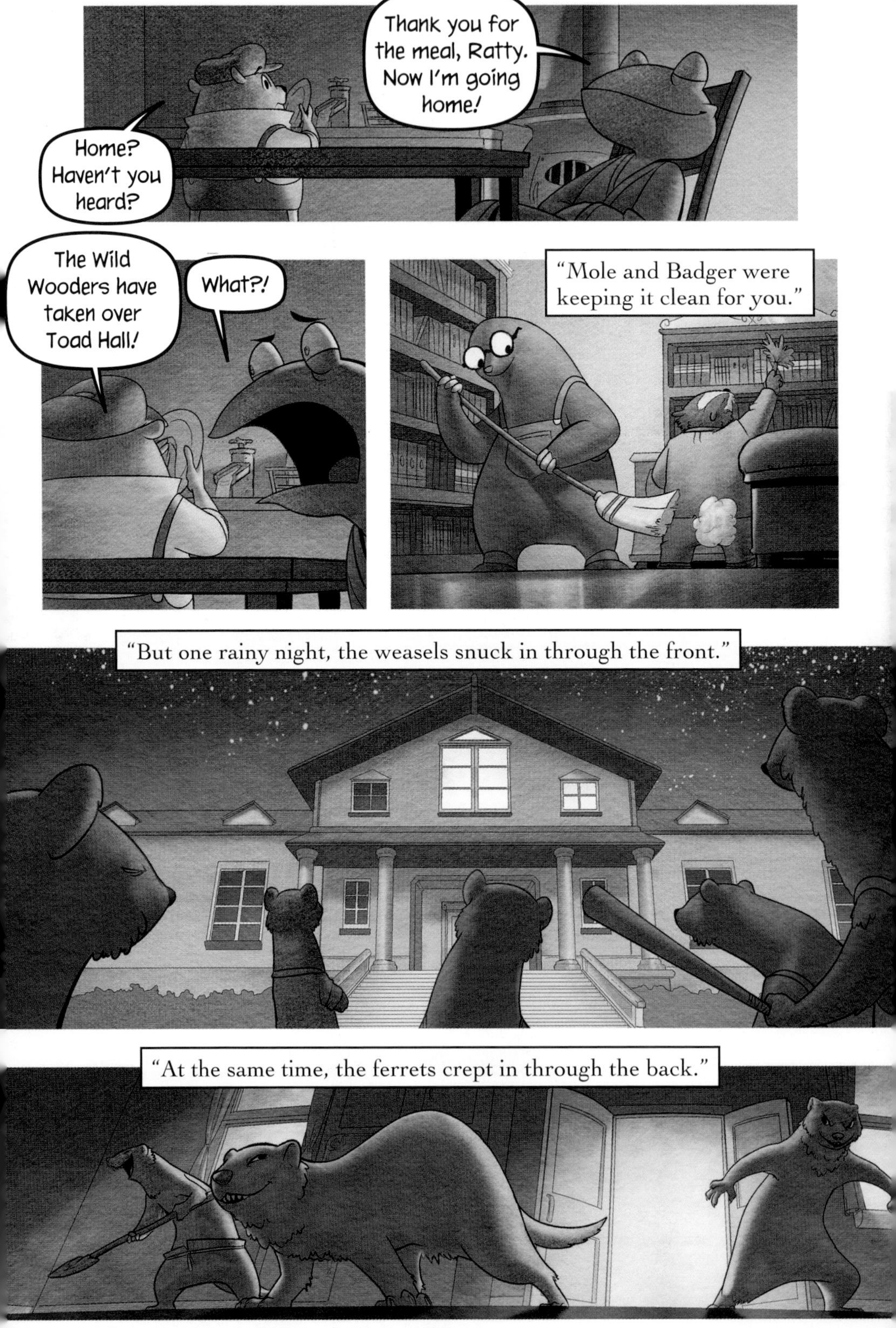
Thank you for the meal, Ratty. Now I'm going home!
Home? Haven't you heard?
The Wild Wooders have taken over Toad Hall!
What?!
"Mole and Badger were keeping it clean for you."
"But one rainy night, the weasels snuck in through the front."
"At the same time, the ferrets crept in through the back."

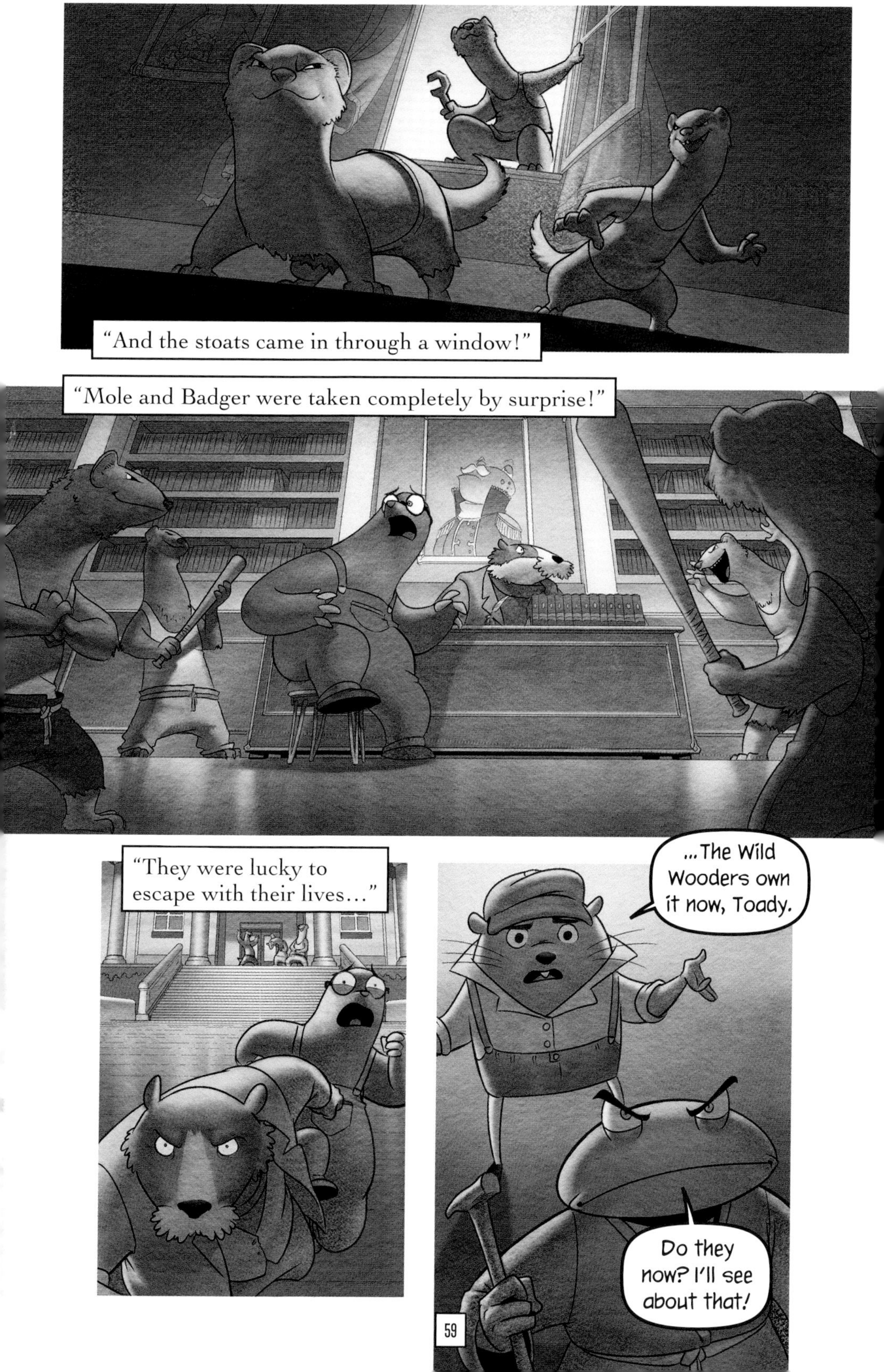
"And the stoats came in through a window!"
"Mole and Badger were taken completely by surprise!"
"They were lucky to escape with their lives..."
...The Wild Wooders own it now, Toady.
Do they now? I'll see about that!

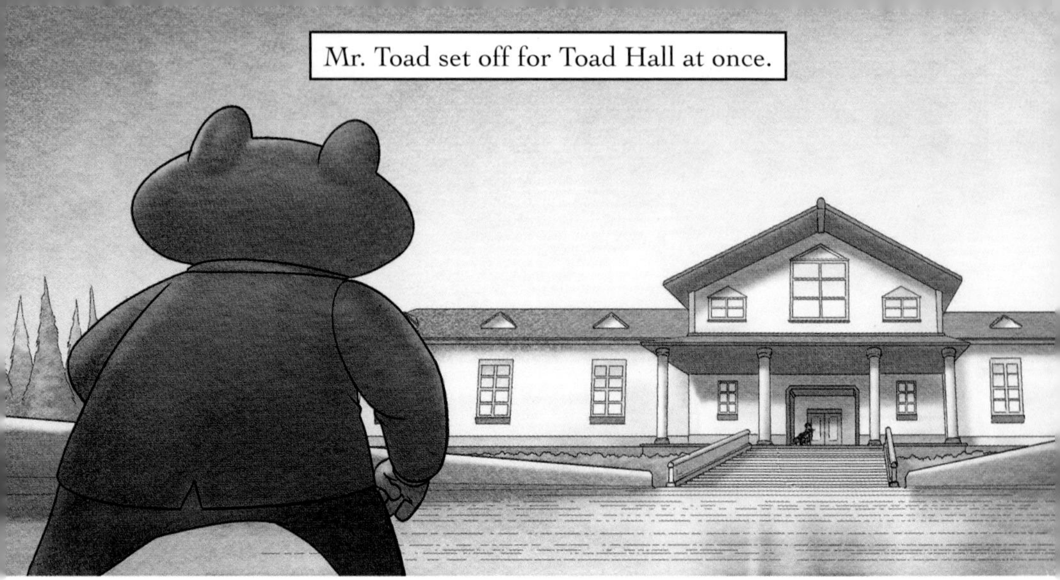
Mr. Toad set off for Toad Hall at once.

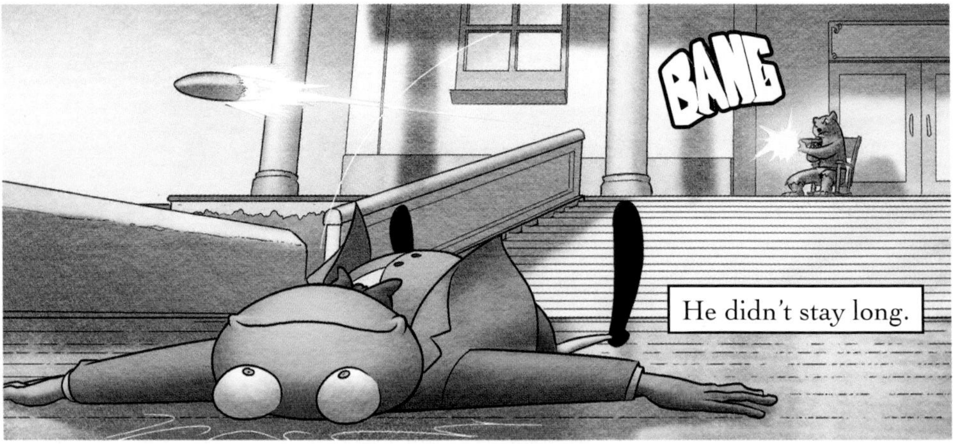
BANG
He didn't stay long.

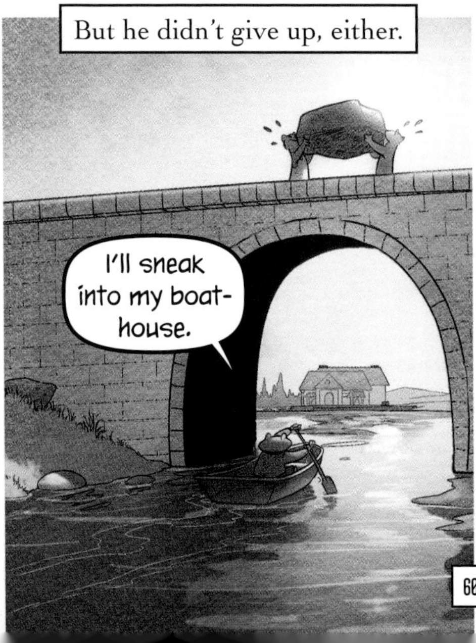
But he didn't give up, either.
I'll sneak into my boat-house.

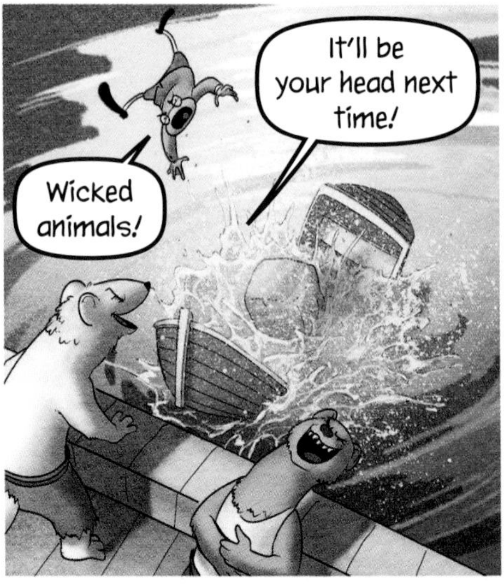
Wicked animals!
It'll be your head next time!

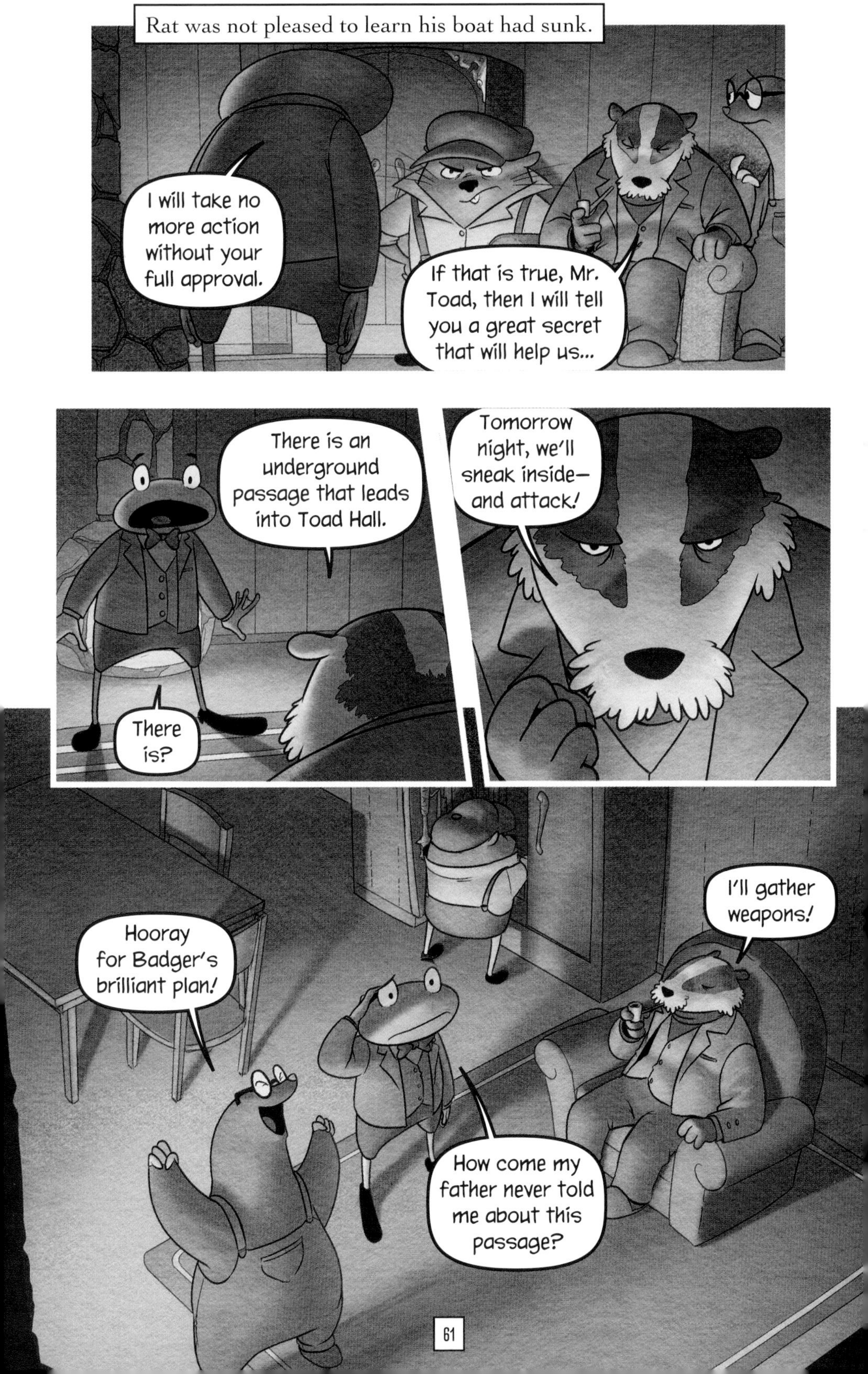
Rat was not pleased to learn his boat had sunk.
I will take no more action without your full approval.
If that is true, Mr. Toad, then I will tell you a great secret that will help us...
There is an underground passage that leads into Toad Hall.
There is?
Tomorrow night, we'll sneak inside—and attack!
Hooray for Badger's brilliant plan!
I'll gather weapons!
How come my father never told me about this passage?

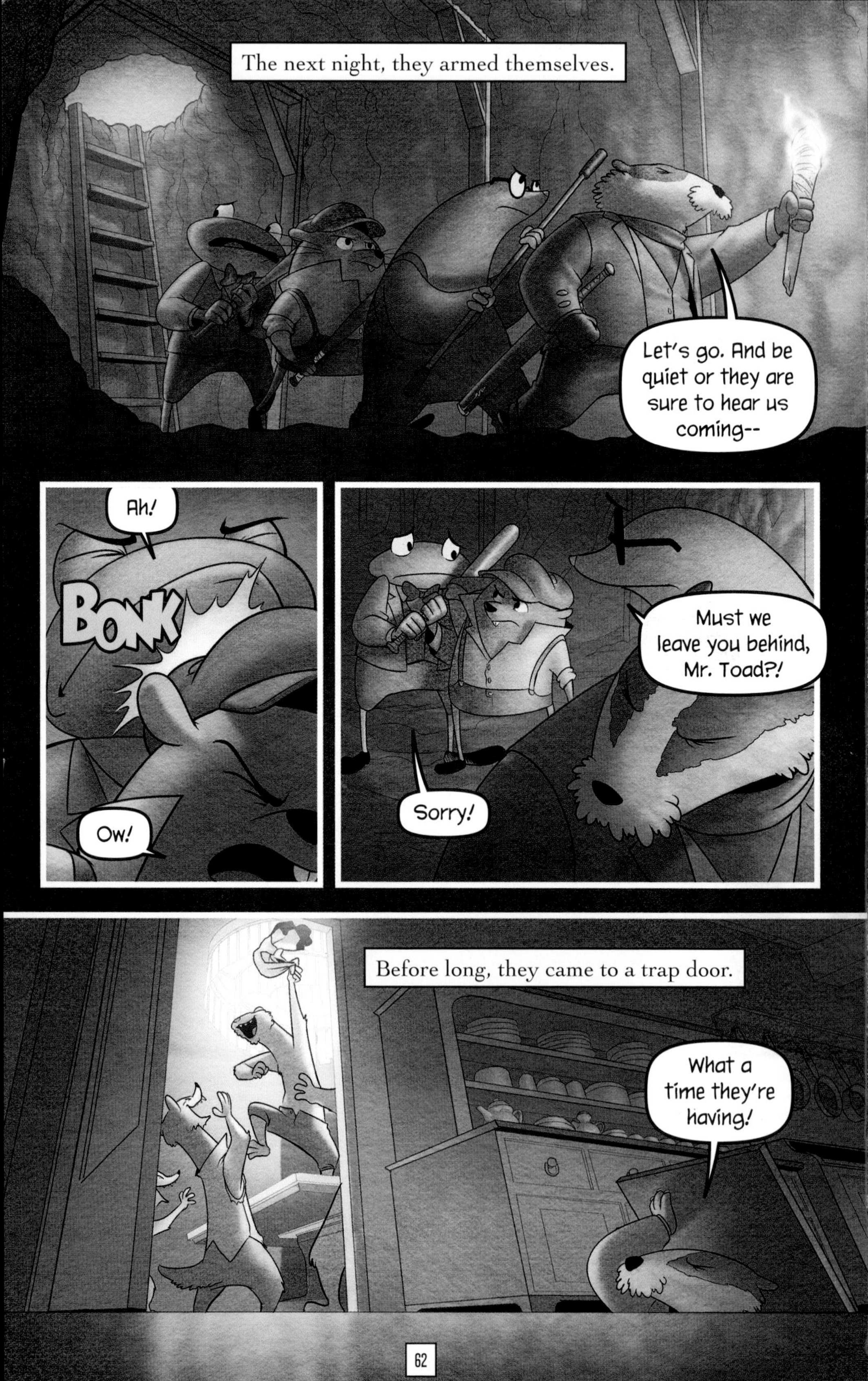
The next night, they armed themselves.
Let's go. And be quiet or they are sure to hear us coming--
Ah!
BONK
Ow!
Must we leave you behind, Mr. Toad?!
Sorry!
Before long, they came to a trap door.
What a time they're having!

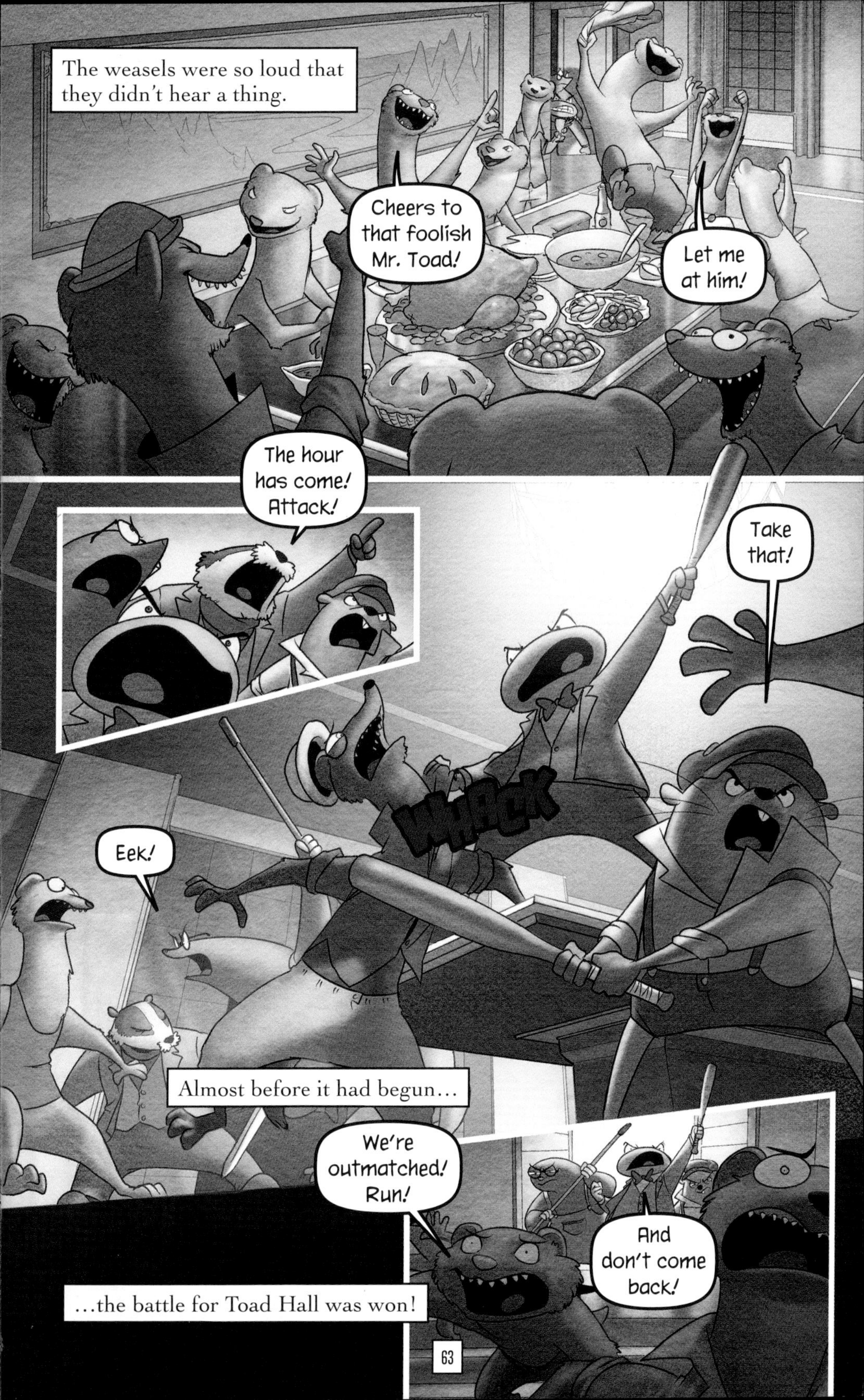
The weasels were so loud that they didn't hear a thing.
Cheers to that foolish Mr. Toad!
Let me at him!
The hour has come! Attack!
Take that!
WHACK
Eek!
Almost before it had begun…
We're outmatched! Run!
And don't come back!
…the battle for Toad Hall was won!

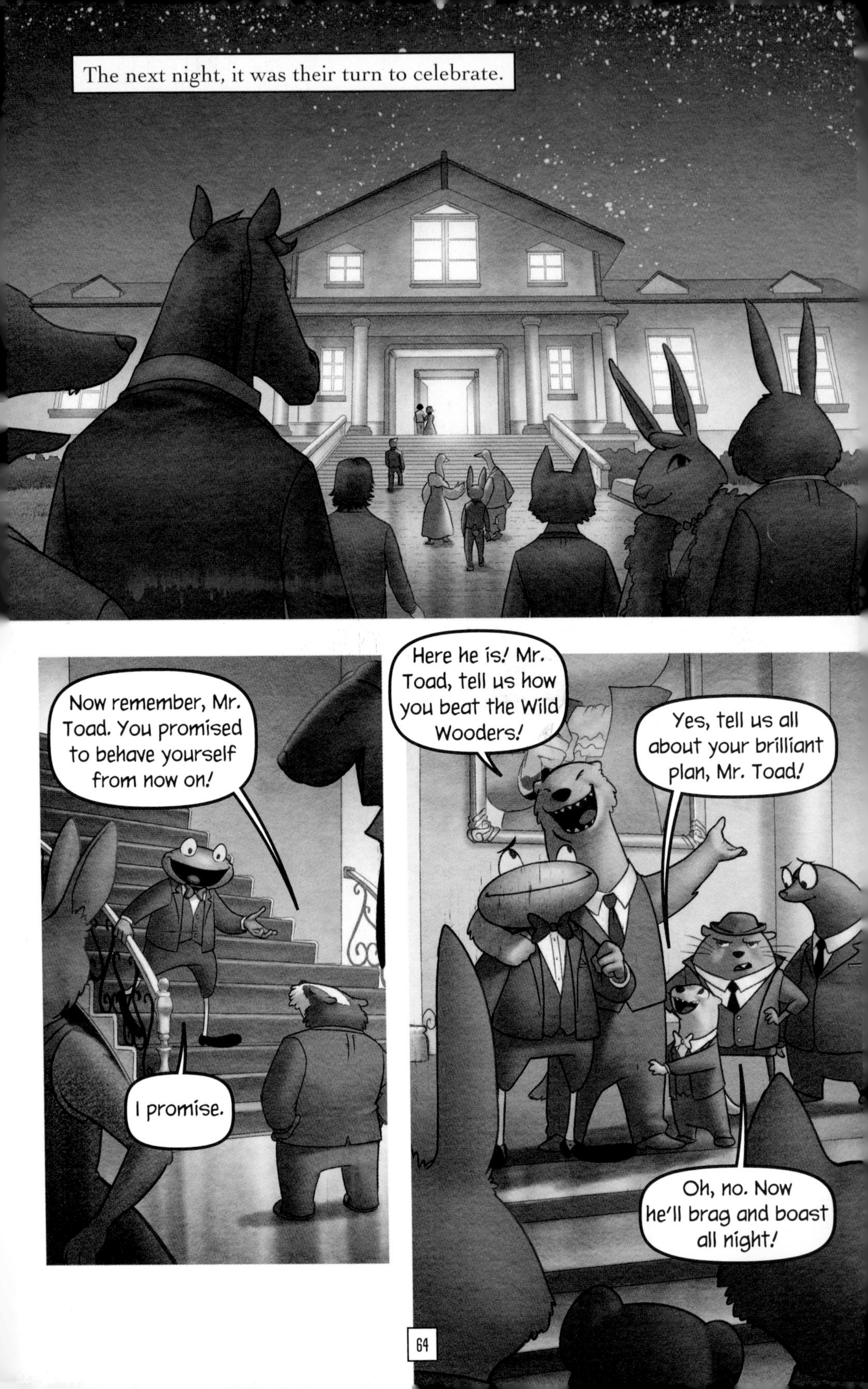
The next night, it was their turn to celebrate.
Now remember, Mr. Toad. You promised to behave yourself from now on!
I promise.
Here he is! Mr. Toad, tell us how you beat the Wild Wooders!
Yes, tell us all about your brilliant plan, Mr. Toad!
Oh, no. Now he'll brag and boast all night!

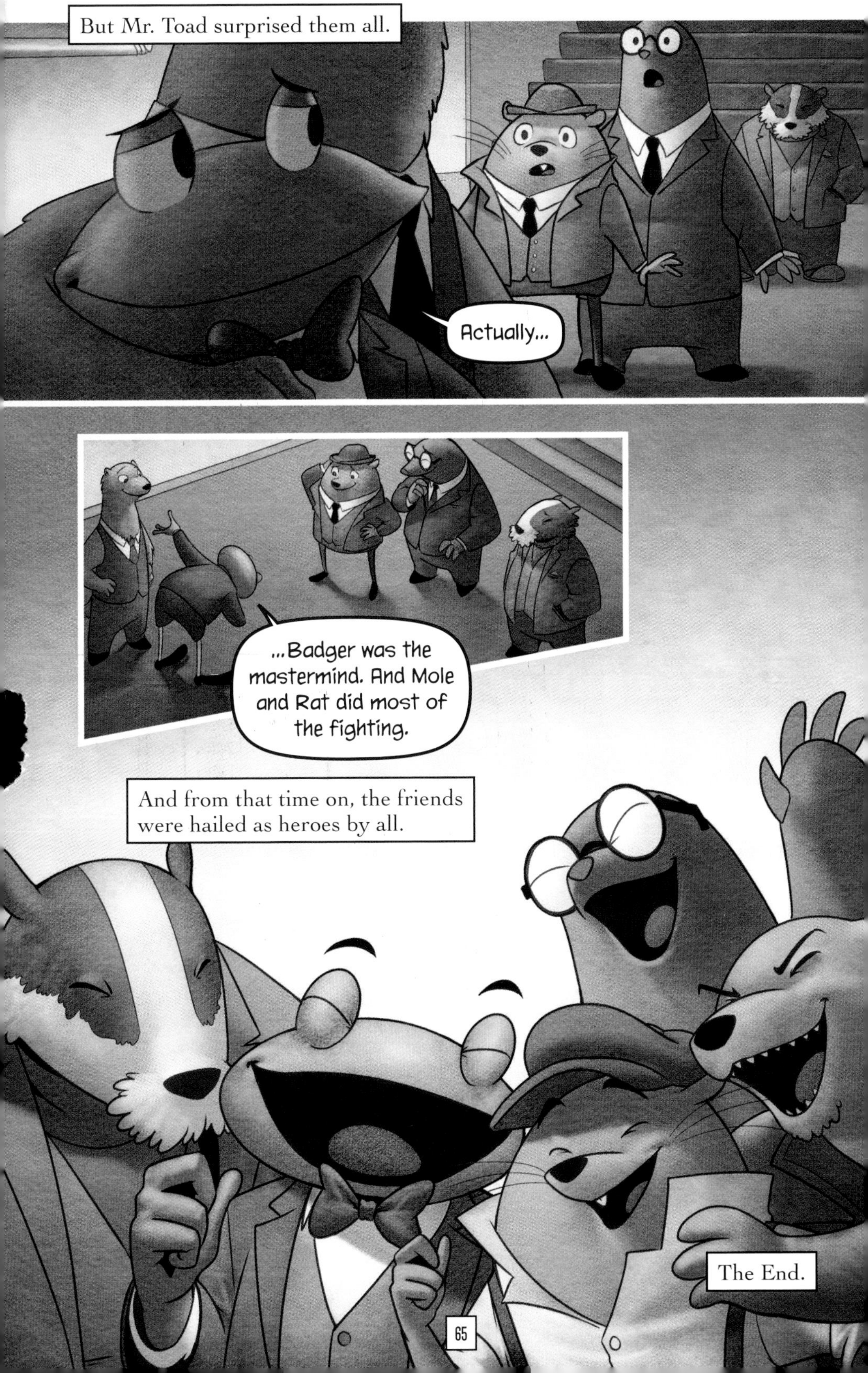
But Mr. Toad surprised them all.
Actually...
...Badger was the mastermind. And Mole and Rat did most of the fighting.
And from that time on, the friends were hailed as heroes by all.
The End.

ABOUT THE RETELLING AUTHOR AND ILLUSTRATOR

After working more than 10 years as a children's book editor, **Stephanie True Peters** started writing books herself. She has since written 40 books, including the New York Times best seller *A Princess Primer: A Fairy Godmother's Guide to Being a Princess*. When not at her computer, Peters enjoys playing with her two children, hitting the gym, or working on home improvement projects with her patient and supportive husband, Daniel.

Fernando Cano is an emerging illustrator born in Mexico City, Mexico. He currently resides in Monterrey, Mexico, where he works as a full-time illustrator and colorist at Graphikslava studio. He has done illustration work for Marvel, DC Comics, and role-playing games like *Pathfinder* from Paizo Publishing. In his spare time, he enjoys hanging out with friends, singing, rowing, and drawing.